By Bruce Clements

Two Against the Tide (1967)

The Face of Abraham Candle (1969)

From Ice Set Free: The Story of Otto Kiep (1972)

I Tell a Lie Every So Often (1974)

Coming Home to a Place You've Never Been Before
with Hanna Clements (1975)

Prison Window, Jerusalem Blue (1977)

Anywhere Else but Here (1980)

Coming About (1984)

The Treasure of Plunderell Manor (1987)

Tom Loves Anna Loves Tom (1990)

A Chapel of Thieves (2002)

What Erika Wants (2005)

What Erika Wants

Bruce Clements

What Erika Wants

Farrar, Straus and Giroux / New York

Distributed in Canada by Douglas & McIntyre Publishing Group
Printed in the United States of America
Designed by Jay Colvin
First edition, 2005
1 3 5 7 9 10 8 6 4 2

www.fsgkidsbooks.com

Library of Congress Cataloging-in-Publication Data
Clements, Bruce.
What Erika wants / Bruce Clements.— 1st ed.
p. cm.
Summary: The bright spot in the life of fourteen-year-old Erika Nevski is her lawyer, who supports Erika as she faces a custody battle, deals with her shoplifting friend, and tries out for the school play.
ISBN-13: 978-0-374-32304-2
ISBN-10: 0-374-32304-6
[1. Family problems—Fiction. 2. Lawyers—Fiction. 3. Actors and actresses—Fiction. 4. Divorce—Fiction.] I. Title.
PZ7.C5912 Wh 2005
[Fic]—dc22
2004056714

The author has donated all his proceeds from the sale of this book to the Children's Law Center of Connecticut, 30 Arbor Street, South Building, Hartford, CT 06106
www.clcct.org

For Judy Hyde, always faithful to children

What Erika Wants

1

The policeman opened the door and Erika stepped out of the courtroom into the hall. "You can't stand right here," he said. "People want to get in and out. You can sit on that bench next to the window."

"I'm sorry," she said. She crossed the hall, put her backpack behind the bench, and stood looking at a bus going down the street.

The policeman followed her. "I'm not arresting you, if that's what you think," he said. "Judge Gifford doesn't want you in there, that's all."

She smiled so he wouldn't think she was mad at him. He was just doing his job.

"I'm fine," she said.

He felt around in his pants pocket, pulled out a bent package of gum, and put it under her nose. "Chew?" he said. "It's okay. It's sugar-free."

She took a step back and sat down. "No. Thank you."

"Pretty bracelets you have."

Erika said nothing.

Two men with briefcases came down the hall and stopped at the elevator. The older one was telling a joke, and the younger one was smiling, waiting for the punch line. She watched them in front of the elevator. It came and they stepped inside. Then, just to have something to do, Erika opened her backpack, got out her algebra workbook, checked inside the cover to make sure the two pages the Stork had given her were still there, and pushed the workbook back inside, careful not to catch it on the torn place in the lining. As she zipped her bag shut and put it back between the bench leg and the wall, the policeman leaned over her. She could smell he was a smoker.

"It's always better out here than it is in there," he said. "I've worked criminal court and I've worked family court. You want to know the difference? In criminal court the worst people act their best, and in family court the best people act their worst. Judge Gifford's probably signing up a lawyer for you right now. It's an honor. How many teenage kids you know have lawyers?"

She thought of Carrie's lawyer, Larry L. Lawrence. "Larry the Loser," Carrie called him. He had been in juvenile court with her four times. Maybe he was a loser, but he had kept her from being sent away to Longmeadow State School.

A woman with round glasses and a black suit pushed open the courtroom door and came across the hall. She had acne scars across her forehead, real pits. She put out her hand. "Erika? My name is Jean Rostow-Kaplan. I'm your lawyer. I'd like it if you called me Jean. Can we go downstairs to the parking lot for a few minutes and talk? There's something in my car I want to give you, and I need to get a little information."

Erika turned away, reached behind the bench, pulled her backpack out, and put it on. When she turned around, the policeman was gone. Jean went to the elevator, pushed the Down button, and they stood side by side waiting for it to come. "Here's what I know already," Jean said. "You can straighten me out where I'm wrong. You live with your father. Your mom was in Arizona until late last year? Is that where she was?"

"Phoenix."

"And we're here because she would like the court to make changes in your current custody arrangements."

"She came back before Christmas. She would have asked for me sooner, but she had to find just the right apartment and everything first."

Jean smiled and nodded. "I know her lawyer. Jack Klecko. He's very good at his job. I don't know if your father has a lawyer or not."

"No, he doesn't." Erika looked back toward the bench, angry at herself. What right did she have to talk about her father to this stranger?

"There was a young woman with your mom," Jean said.

"My sister, Karen."

"Mr. Klecko said your mom had a child from her first marriage. Is that Karen?"

"I don't think of her that way. She's just my sister," Erika said. She looked at the elevator door. Why wasn't it coming? Was the old lawyer holding the door open on the first floor, still telling his joke? It was possible.

Jean shifted her briefcase from her right hand to her left. "You got a glimpse of Judge Gifford," she said. "He's the best there is. He stays awake nights getting at the truth."

Erika remembered an experiment she had done one Saturday morning years ago. Take identical bowls, write the letter *C* on the bottom of one with a crayon, put true Cheerios and milk in that bowl, store-brand Cheerios and milk in the other, shut your eyes and move the bowls around until you don't know which is which, then take a spoon and try to figure out which is the true one. It was hard, and when she made her choice it didn't have a *C* on the bottom.

Jean reached out and pushed the Down button again. "They always take a long time," she said. "Let me tell you a little bit more about me. I'm an attorney, as you know. I work for the Children's Law Center on Orchard Street.

Seven or eight blocks on the other side of the interstate. The center pays me a salary, so you or your parents won't ever get a bill. My job is to keep you informed about what's happening with your case, to give you advice, which you can take or not, as you decide, and to argue in court for what you want."

The elevator came and they stepped inside. Jean pushed the ground-floor button and the doors slowly slid shut. When she turned to Erika and spoke, there was a slight echo. "Whatever you say to me is confidential, unless you tell me you're planning to rob a bank, which doesn't seem likely."

Erika tried not to smile. What kind of idiot would tell her lawyer she was going to rob a bank?

"We have two other lawyers. Sometimes I ask them for their ideas on how to help a client. I hope that's okay."

"Sure," Erika said.

The elevator stopped, the door opened, and Jean started down the hall toward the door out to the parking lot. Erika had to walk fast to catch up. "Does my mom know where we're going?" she asked.

"I told her she could meet you on the front steps of the courthouse in fifteen minutes," Jean said. She led the way past the security guard, who gave her a little salute, and then out the door and across the lot. The sun was setting between the courthouse and the main post office, and the wind was cold. Erika had her sweatshirt balled up in her backpack, so she was glad when they got inside Jean's car, an old Dodge with rust spots on the doors. An empty plastic bag blew against the windshield, caught on a wiper blade for a second, and then flew away.

Looking through the windshield, Erika saw her mom and Karen come out of the courthouse door and stand at the top of the stairs. Her mom was wearing a blue dress and a string of pearls. The dress was a little tight on her. Mr. Klecko came out behind them, then walked around and stood in front of her, waving his arms and talking in her face. It made Erika want to jump out of the car and run across the lot and up the stairs three at a time, grab him and stop him. Men who waved their arms and yelled shouldn't be allowed to be lawyers, or if they were allowed, they should be allowed to work only for guilty people who had done really bad things, not for moms who just wanted to get their children back home.

Jean had thrown her briefcase onto the backseat and was feeling around under a pile of newspapers, candy wrappers, sweatshirts, and soccer equipment. "I'm sorry this is taking so long," she said. She grabbed what she was looking for and swung around holding it up in the air. It was a diary with a picture of a log cabin on the cover. In front of the cabin a woman washed clothes in a tub, a man chopped wood, and a little boy and girl played with a dog. Smoke curled up from the chimney.

"This might be useful to you," Jean said, "or it might not. It's for writing down what you're thinking, how you're feeling, ideas, things you want to remember, things you want me to do."

"Thank you."

Erika tried not to stare at the acne scars on Jean's forehead. They made her think of Candice Boyle. In eighth grade Candice hadn't had any, and now she was the pimple queen of Hoover Junior High. She had them everywhere, even on her shoulders. Some kids said it was a sign she was taking steroids to make her better at basketball.

Jean handed the diary to her. "I won't ever ask to look at it, so I won't know if you write in it or not, but you might be glad to have it to help you remember later."

Erika nodded her head and shifted her body around so she was leaning against the passenger door.

"The picture on the front's a little hokey," Jean said. "I bought a box of twenty four of them at the Christmas Tree Shop on Cape Cod last year for a dollar apiece. I couldn't resist. I love diaries. I kept one when I was in sixth grade. I made believe I was writing letters to a friend who had moved away to California. I even began to believe in her."

Erika knew what she was talking about. For a long time her friend Carrie had had a make-believe friend named Bonnie. Sometimes when Carrie's mom was driving them to the mall or somewhere, Carrie would bend over and ask Bonnie a question and then tilt her head and listen for the answer. A lot of times Bonnie would give her ideas of different things to do, and she'd do them. It drove Mrs. Ives crazy.

Erika looked toward the courthouse door. Jack Klecko was gone and Karen was running down the stairs. She must have asked Bernie to drive them home. Sell the right stuff, or better yet get other guys to sell it for you so they're the ones to get arrested and sent to jail, and you can afford to pay cash for a Jaguar.

"May I?" Jean asked. She took back the diary and opened the rear cover. "I'm putting down the address and phone number of the Children's Law Center. The second number is my cell phone, which I never turn off except in movies and at church. Please don't let anyone else have it, not even your parents. I'm going to be in touch with them soon and give them my office number. Access to my cell phone belongs only to my husband, my children, and my clients. Nobody else."

An ambulance went by the entrance to the parking lot with its lights flashing but no siren. Jean closed the diary and gave it back, and Erika stowed it in her backpack.

"They're not going to hold it against Mom for bringing me, are they?" she asked. "It's just that she wanted me to see what was happening."

Jean reached her hand out but stopped before she touched her. "It's a simple misunderstanding about the rules. Judge Gifford saw what had happened, decided to assign me to you, and moved on to other things. It won't get in the way of the case. It can be helpful to have your own lawyer. You can call me day or night. I like to get calls from clients, and my husband can sleep through anything."

"Are most of them around my age?" Erika asked.

Jean smiled. "You're old. A lot of my clients are five and six. Three, some. When they're that young, I usually get appointed guardian. I go to court and say what I think is best for them and why, and the judge decides. When I'm the attorney, the children tell me what they want, and I try to get it for them."

Erika wondered if Jean really believed that. A lot of adults believed what they said about themselves. Mr. Janik, her guidance counselor, thought he knew everything about every kid in the ninth grade. He also thought they all loved him. Amazing. Still, he was better than the ones who told you they wanted you to be free to choose for yourself, but really just wanted to push their plans for you.

"I know what I want," she said.

"You don't need to tell me what it is right away," Jean said. "It'll be at least November or December before Judge Gifford rules. You have plenty of time."

"I want to go home to Mom," she said. "I mean, I'd still see my dad every week, but I'd live at home. My dad's really great. Every year he bakes me a birthday cake."

Jean looked at a paper in her briefcase. "October twenty-first you'll be fifteen," she said. "Is it the same flavor cake every year?"

"Chocolate." Erika took hold of the door handle and rubbed her thumb back and forth on it, but then pulled her hand away and put it down between the seat and the door. She didn't want this woman to think she was in a hurry to go. She looked toward the courthouse. Mom was still standing at the top of the stairs waiting for her.

Jean took a legal form out of her briefcase and held it out so Erika could see it. Halfway down, under all the names and seals, were the words MOTION FOR MODIFICATION OF CUSTODY. She saw her mom's quick, scrawly signature on the bottom.

"Just so I'm certain," Jean said, "is this address and phone number for your mom still correct?"

"Yes."

Jean lifted the form. Underneath was a small square of yellow paper. "And this is your father's home number? Is there a way I can reach him at work?"

She handed a pencil to Erika, who hesitated a second and then wrote the number on the paper. "It's Pace Brothers' Ford," she said. "They're the biggest Ford dealership in the eastern half of the state. He's assistant manager in the body shop. You have to ask for him."

Jean put the papers in a folder, put the folder back in her briefcase, and looked at Erika's mom standing at the courthouse door. Erika prayed that Bernie wouldn't come running up the stairs where Jean could see him. You could tell a mile away he was bad news.

"Will your mom be dropping you off at your dad's?" Jean asked.

"No. I'm taking the bus. It's easier." Erika pushed the door open an inch. Cold wind blew into the car.

"One last thing before you go," Jean said. "I need to make an appointment with you. I'm in court all day tomorrow. Would next Monday or Tuesday work?"

"There are tryouts for the school play both days."

"Are you an actress?"

"All I've been is on stage crew so far, but Mr. Stork makes a big thing of the way you look. He needs somebody tall with long hair, and there aren't too many ninth graders like that, so he gave me some lines he wants me to be ready to read. I don't know if I will."

"I think you should."

How would you know? Erika thought.

"When does the play go on?" Jean asked.

"In forty-two days. I know because the Stork already has a countdown sign on his door. He thinks it helps sell tickets. I guess it was silly, but I thought the judge would decide everything today."

"Court business never moves fast," Jean said. "I need to know a lot more than I do now. So, if you tried out Monday, would you be free to see me Tuesday? Maybe around four-thirty?"

Erika got out of the car. "I guess so. Sure."

Jean took out another piece of paper, a map with the law

center in the middle of it and the bus lines marked, wrote "Tuesday, 10/11, 4:30 p.m.," across the top, and handed it to her. "Maybe you could bring pictures of the people in your family with you? You think that might be possible?"

Erika smiled, opened the door all the way, got out, slammed the door, waved goodbye, and started moving between the cars toward her mother, walking fast. Halfway there, with the paper flapping around in her hand, she stopped. There was one more thing she needed to say. She put the map in her pocket and went back. When she got near the car, Jean rolled down her window and put her head out.

Erika brushed her hair out of her eyes. "Just one other thing," she said. "I didn't just decide today about wanting to go home. I've been wanting to go home ever since my mom and my sister came back from Arizona last year. Before that. Always, really. Also, I don't think anybody should hold it against Mom for bringing me into court. She just wanted me to be able to see what was happening."

Jean smiled up at her. "Don't worry. It's no big deal." Her cell phone, lying on the passenger seat, began to ring. She picked it up and checked the caller ID, then put it on the seat again. Erika looked down at it.

"It's not a client, so I don't need to answer right away," Jean said.

Erika shook her head. "No, that's okay, I'm going," she said. "You can call the person back if you want."

Erika crossed the lot and ran up the courthouse stairs. When she got to the top, her mom grabbed her and put her mouth to her ear. "Tell me the truth now, sweetie. You're not mad at me for bringing you, right? You got a lawyer out of it. That's something. Or maybe you don't want one."

"It's fine." Erika looked around. "Where's Karen?"

"Gone to find Bernie. You can have a ride, too, if you want. There's plenty of room. Don't tell Karen, but sometimes I think Bernie likes you best of all of us."

Erika shook her head. He was a snake. He hated her as much as she hated him. At least, she hoped he did.

"Suit yourself," her mom said. "You're a big girl now. Are you sure you're not mad at me for taking you into the courtroom? I don't think the judge liked me. Do you think I put on too much eyeliner? Karen says I did, but maybe she's just mad at me because I borrowed hers. You don't have to tell her that, okay? It goes on like a dream. Remember when you were little, telling me my eyes looked spooky?"

"No," Erika said.

"Well, you did. Moms remember little hurts like that. We can't help ourselves. You think that's the real reason he gave you a lawyer? How I looked?"

Erika shook her head. "I'm sure that wasn't it, Mom."

"That courtroom's like a church," her mom said, fluttering her hand at the building. "The ceiling must be three stories high. The words just flew up there and got lost. You probably couldn't hear a word anybody said. Whatever happened, I don't care as long as you don't think I did something wrong taking you there. Not that there was anything wrong. What could be wrong about wanting your daughter to know what's going on? Of course, if your father keeps hiding in that auto body shop instead of showing up, we won't ever be able to do anything. Maybe you can get your lawyer to do something, file a paper or something, to get him there when he's supposed to be. He never faces facts, ever. So what happens? You end up getting led away by that policeman and having to stand out in the hall, where everybody going by can stare at you and think you're a criminal or something when you're the best girl in the world. It's really all your daddy's fault. Anyway, there's no use talking about it. No harm done. Is that your lawyer's car still in the parking lot? It looks kind of junky, doesn't it? What's her name?"

"Jean," Erika said. "That's what she wants me to call her."

Her mom turned her mouth down. "She said for you to use her first name? She can't be much of a lawyer if she's in such a hurry to be your buddy. Maybe I should go over and visit with her. I wanted to have a little talk with her in the courtroom, but I could see the judge didn't want me to."

Karen came running up the steps. She had a worried look on her small, round face.

"Bernie's here. We've got to go. You know how he hates to wait. I'll see you in the car. Don't just stand there, hurry. He's doing us a big favor. He's got business to do. Please. Okay?"

Her mom paid no attention. "So, what are we going to do about your father?" she asked. "You know how he is, he doesn't do anything and he doesn't do anything and he doesn't do anything and then all of a sudden he blows up or starts crying like a baby. You've got to treat him like one. I know. Don't let him throw one of his famous little tantrums. Just soften him up. Get him ready for what's going to happen. Of course, the only one who can really change him is him, and what are the chances of that? Zero. It's too bad, when you think of it, but let's face it, it's all his own fault."

Bernie beeped his horn. Karen shut her eyes tight. "Please, right now," she said.

Her mom smiled. "Bernie bought a new car in honor of your homecoming," she said. "German. No, English. Not a Rolls-Royce but the other kind. We used to see a lot of them in Phoenix. Cost him a bundle of money. The backseat's too hard, though. Not much room for your long legs, but you could sit in front and Karen could sit in back with me. She wouldn't mind. She wanted him to get it in fire engine red, but he and I both thought gunmetal gray was better. What do you think?"

"I don't know," Erika said.

"How can you know when you're not even looking that way? Anyway, about Saturday morning, you have to come early. Let the big baby make his own breakfast. Put a box of cereal on the kitchen table and take off and we'll wait for you and the three of us will have a big traditional Saturday morning breakfast, okay?"

Erika didn't want to promise. "Did I tell you yet? I'm thinking about trying out for the school play."

Bernie beeped again. Karen ran down the stairs to him.

"You sure you have enough time?" her mom asked. "Can you, with all the other things you've got on your plate? You're a young lady now, so naturally you have to decide for yourself, but do you really think you can do it?"

"It's not for six weeks," Erika said.

"Well, all right," her mom said. "You'll be home by then, and I can help you put your makeup on. Another good thing, it'll make Courtney jealous. Show her she doesn't own you."

"It's Carrie. She's my best friend."

Her mom stuck out her tongue and waggled her head. "See you early Saturday." She ran down to the car, pulled open the door and got in, and the car drove away. As soon as it was out of sight, Erika opened her backpack, took her sweatshirt out, and put it on. Then she went down the stairs and stood waiting by the parking lot exit. She thought about the scars on Jean's forehead. Most women would have found some way of covering them up, combing their hair so it looped across, or wearing bangs, but Jean had her hair parted in the center and pulled back as if to say, "Here I am, scars and all, take me or leave me."

Jean sat sorting out the papers in her briefcase, deciding what she could leave in the office and what she needed to take home and study after the kids were in bed. When she was done she drove to the parking lot exit. Erika was waiting for her. Jean pulled to the side so as not to block the gate, and Erika walked over. The late afternoon sun made her blowing hair flash red.

"I'm sorry to stop you," she said.

"That's fine. Actually, I just remembered that when I called my husband I didn't remind him to pick up our son Nathan after his trumpet lesson, so I had to stop anyway."

"It's about my dad." Erika heard the bus and turned her head to look toward the street. The bus stopped, picked up two passengers, and drove off trailing a cloud of black smoke.

"They run every ten minutes," Jean said. "You want to get in and watch for the next one? I'm not in that much of a hurry."

Erika smiled. "That's okay, I'm fine," she said. "I was just wondering about what my father might start thinking."

"He doesn't need to worry about not being here today," Jean said. "Nothing's going to happen without his input. Judge Gifford doesn't work that way."

"It's not that," Erika said. "It's just that when I tell him about getting a lawyer, he might think it's all of a sudden four against one. I mean, he already knows about Mom and her lawyer, and when I tell him I've got one, he might think people are ganging up on him."

"I could call him at work and tell him it's not your fault, that you couldn't say no, you didn't want me," Jean said.

"Shall I do that? I need to make an appointment with him anyway."

"Okay," Erika said. "He's working late tonight. Can I tell you one more thing?"

"You can always tell your attorney one more thing," Jean said.

"I guess I already have. I think a girl should be home with her mom. It's probably the best thing for both of them." She shifted the straps on her backpack. "Well, okay, I'll see you Tuesday."

Jean put her left hand out and stopped short just before she reached Erika's arm. "We'll do our best to see the right thing's done," she said, and watched Erika go to the bus stop. Then she called her husband and found out he was already parked across the street from the trumpet teacher's house. Driving out through the gate, she waved at Erika, who smiled and waved back. Did the girl have any idea how beautiful she was? Probably not.

When Jean got back to the Children's Law Center, which was on the first floor of an old factory building, everybody had gone home. She turned on the lights in the reception area, put the Erika Nevski case folder on Kit's desk, slapped a sticky note on it, and wrote, "Kit, intake papers to M. and D. Thanks." Then she went down the hall into her office. There was a phone message from Jack Klecko. She had known Jack from the time they both worked for the housing authority, before he went into divorce law and she started working for the law center. On her last case at the H.A. she and Jack had been a team. She had recovered three sisters from an uncle who had taken them to Florida, and Jack had worked out a way for their mother to stay in a two-bedroom apartment in public housing until the kids were back.

There were two things she didn't like about Jack. The first was that he used the same line, "See what I'm saying?" over and over again, making it into one word, "Seewumsane?" The second was that he always talked as if he owned his clients. Back when they were both working at the H.A. he would say "my tenants" and "my building" and "my landlord." Now that he was doing divorce cases he would say "my wife," "my husband," and "my separation agreement." She sat down and dialed his number.

He picked the phone up on the second ring. "Jack Klecko," he said. He had a loud barroom voice, as if he were talking to you in the middle of a noisy crowd.

"Jack. It's Jean. You left a message for me to call you."

"Right," he said. "I already told you some stuff in court, right?"

"A little," Jean said.

"Anyway," he said, "the important thing I want you to know is what a very special, close relationship is going on between my mom and Erika. She probably told you about it when you talked to her, right?"

"We had a nice talk," Jean said.

"Sure you did," Jack said. "Why not? My mom's nice, the girl's nice. Sitting her down in the courtroom wasn't my idea. You know that, right? When my mom told me she wanted to do it, I told her there was no way it would help her, but she did it anyway. Your clients do things on their own. Seewumsane?"

"Don't worry about it," Jean said. "Her daughter apologized for her, by the way."

"Erika? Really? She didn't need to do that."

"She thought she did."

"Nice girl. Anyway, I chewed my mom out for it. I saw you sitting in your car after, so you probably saw me doing it. If Erika hadn't been that tall, Judge Gifford probably wouldn't have paid attention to her. Well, maybe he would have. I'm sure you weren't looking for another case, but this one's easy. Everybody lives in the same city, for one thing. That's a big plus. Simple. My mom wants her little girl to *come* home, her little girl wants to *go* home. And you know how redheads are. They know what they want and you better not stand in their way, seewumsane?"

"Auburn," Jean said.

There was silence at his end for a few seconds. "What?"

"Auburn," Jean said. "She isn't a true redhead. Her hair's more auburn. The afternoon light made it look redder than it is."

"Right. Sure. Okay. Anyway, all we need to do is get my mom's ex in line and we're home free, seewumsane? A girl should be with her mother. Everybody knows that. And my mom loves this girl with her whole heart. You can see that a mile away. Erika'd have her own room, and her sister's there for company. I don't remember her name. There's ten years between them. Karen. That's her name. Karen. You know the father's *pro se*? Says he can't afford a lawyer, so he's going to represent himself. Poor fish. My mom had to go to Arizona for her health and they called it abandonment. Ridiculous."

Jean looked at her watch. It was almost five-thirty, and she had to stop at the supermarket on her way home and she hadn't decided what to fix for dinner yet. "So, is there anything else you need to talk to me about?" she asked. "I told Brian and the kids I'd cook something special. I've got one more call and the shopping to do."

"Did you notice her bracelets?" Jack asked. "Native American goods from Arizona. All from my mom. Sent one every Christmas, and brought the fourth one back for last Christmas. No question there's a bond between those two. As far as I know, the dad doesn't do anything for her, seewumsane? Okay. Well, goodbye. Just keep in mind, it's a simple case. Judge Gifford won't hear it until the middle of November probably, but we could work it out way before then, seewumsane? Goodbye."

After hanging up, Jean dialed Mr. Nevski's number and asked for the body shop. A man answered.

"Mr. Nevski?" she said.

"Right."

"My name is Jean Rostow-Kaplan. I'm calling to introduce myself. Judge Gifford of family court decided this afternoon to give your daughter Erika a lawyer, and he appointed me. I work for the Children's Law Center. I wanted to let you know as soon as possible."

"Okay."

"Perhaps we could meet sometime, at your convenience," she said.

"Okay," he said again, and then there was a pause. "Why?"

"I need to know about Erika's family, the people who are important to her."

"Sure. Okay," he said. "We'll talk sometime. Goodbye."

At eleven, Erika stood in the doorway between the kitchen and the living room watching her father watching football, the Cowboys against the Giants. He was a big Giants fan, and she usually liked to sit with him and watch their games, but not tonight. She went back to the kitchen table to finish the last steps in an algebra problem, but she kept glancing at her father on the couch. Had Jean called him at work? He hadn't said anything when he came in, just turned on the game.

After a while she got up and went into the bathroom and looked in the mirror and checked her forehead for pimples starting. Then she turned her head a little to the right and examined the left side of her nose. Mrs. Droste had told her in fifth grade that her profile was "classic." She turned left and leaned toward the mirror. Would she go to a plastic surgeon and get her nose trimmed down someday if she could? No. It was beaky, but it wasn't *that* beaky. She decided the next time she was in a drugstore to buy some strong anti-pimple cream.

She heard her father coming down the hall, took a last look at her face, and opened the door. "It's all yours," she said. She went into the kitchen, looked over her algebra homework, and then turned to the back of the workbook. Her answer was right, but it had taken her twelve steps when it was only supposed to take seven. Mrs. Meigs always took off a third if your method was wrong.

Erika took the phone into her bedroom and called Carrie to talk her into trying out for the play.

"Not in a million years," Carrie said. "You do it if you want. The Stork wants you to be a star, so be one. You want it too, right?"

Erika didn't know what to say. Maybe she did want to be a star. "I probably won't try out, either," she said. "And if I do, I won't get the part, but if you tried out, I would, too."

"You know why I'm not? For openers, the name. Footlighters. It's so stupid. It's like out of the fifties or something. Back when they had little tiny black-and-white televisions and kids went to sock hops."

"What are sock hops?"

"You went to the gym and took off one shoe and threw it

onto a pile and then had a free-for-all and whoever got your shoe you had to fight off all night. It stank. Maybe they didn't care back then."

Erika looked up as her father walked in, picked up her clock from her dresser, pointed to it, smiled a quick smile, and put it back down again. The only time he smiled for more than two seconds in a row was when he was working on his car and had his fingers in some tight spot most men wouldn't be able to reach. He had a towel over his right shoulder, and his face was bright red. He always shaved just before he went to bed so he wouldn't have to in the morning.

Erika smiled at him. "Daddy's here," she said into the phone. "He wants me to turn off my light."

"Call me back at midnight," Carrie said, "and I'll tell you the real reason for me not being in the play. If you don't, I'm going to call you. Do what you always do when you want to stay awake, worry about your mom."

Erika hung up the phone and looked at her father. "How's the game going?"

"It's a blowout," he said. "The Giants are down thirty-one to three. That was Carrie, right? What do you see in her? She's not your type."

"We've been friends since fifth grade," Erika said.

Her father shook his head. "Friends do things for you," he said. "She doesn't. She just talks and makes you listen."

"We take turns," Erika said.

"She decides whose turn it is," he said. "Right? Right? Done with your homework?"

"I have to study some more," she said. "There's an algebra test tomorrow." She took a deep breath. "Mom took me with her to court today and the judge gave me a lawyer. The lawyer said she might call you, but maybe she didn't do it."

"You don't trust her to keep her word?" he asked.

Erika shrugged. "I don't know her that well," she said. "Did she?"

"Call me? Yeah. How'd you get there?"

"Bus."

"How'd she get there?"

"Mom? By car, I guess."

"Whose?" he asked. "That guy's, right?"

Erika shrugged. "I think they thought you'd probably be there."

He felt in his pants pockets. "Yeah, well, I got some legal paper in the mail a long time ago. I showed you and told you to remind me."

Her face felt hot. Had he told her? She didn't think so.

He took his long hands out of his pockets. "At least I put it on the kitchen table for you to look at," he said.

"I don't think so."

"Okay. Whatever. I had it open on the kitchen table for a while. I've still got it somewhere. Probably in yesterday's pants. I couldn't have gone anyway. Four jobs came in. Fender benders, but still I had all kinds of work just figuring out where in the yard to put them. Don't worry, I found out about your lawyer. She called and told me. She says she's going to call me again so I can see her. Maybe she will, maybe she won't. You want her?"

Erika shrugged her shoulders. "I don't know. She's free."

"Nobody's free. From the way she talks, she sounds like she comes from New York. What's her name? She told me. I don't remember."

"Jean Rostow-Kaplan."

"Whatever. I'm going to finish watching the game. I could still make the point spread." He came over, kissed her on top of the head, and picked up the phone on her night table. "I know you're thinking of calling Carrie back. Don't. She's not worth your time. The lawyer probably isn't, either, come to think of it."

He left her door open. The volume on their old TV kept jumping up and down. Each time, her dad got out of his chair and stomped across the living room and banged on the top of it. She put her pajamas on, took her new diary out of her backpack, shut the door, and sat on the edge of her bed thinking.

Her mom was right. It was sad, but Daddy didn't know how to deal with any kind of change. He had been shocked when she started liking mushrooms on her half of the pizza. When anything happened he didn't expect, he'd suddenly get real quiet, and then you knew he was either going to start crying or explode. He wouldn't like her having a lawyer. Lawyers went to court. Lawyers changed things. She climbed under the covers, opened her diary, and began to write.

Dear Diary,

OK, don't worry, I'm really not crazy.

What if they built this orange juice factory that could squeeze only one orange at a time? What would it feel like if you were <u>the</u> orange of the day? All that machinery just for you.

<u>IT'S 42 DAYS TO OPENING NIGHT.</u>

I still might not try out. I haven't promised anybody. Even if I only get on the stage crew it's still the same number.

Daddy knows not to look at my stuff, but still I'm going to put you in my suitcase and lock you up.

Love,

Erika

She pulled her suitcase out from under the bureau and unlocked it. The only thing in it was a letter Karen had sent Erika last year complaining about Mom and telling Erika it was time for her to begin pulling her weight. It was true, but it wasn't something for her father to read, even by accident. She put the diary on top of the letter, locked the suitcase, and pushed it back under the bureau.

At midnight, she went to the kitchen and got the phone.

Her dad was sitting on the couch with a can of beer. He grinned at her. "I made the spread," he said. "For ten dollars I made eighteen fifty. Not bad."

Erika said good night, went back to bed, and dialed Carrie's number. Carrie answered on the first ring.

"I knew you'd call," she said.

"I wanted to tell you," Erika said. "I got a lawyer. The judge gave her to me."

"Lawyers are nothing special. Remember Larry the Loser?"

"From the way she talks, I think she's from New York. Daddy thinks so, too."

"So, you want to know the real reason I'm not going to star in the play? I'll tell you. It's because I see through people, which people know, which makes them scared of me. People like me who can see through people are always someplace they aren't, so I can't be touched. All the time, even when I'm sleeping or on the toilet, I'm really all the time in this other country, and nobody else can get there because they're stuck in the same country everybody else in the world is stuck in twenty-four-seven. I talked to the Stork yesterday. He puffed up the way he does and said acting in a play is like being in another country, as if that was big news. I don't need that because I'm already in one. In fact, I *am* one. Are you falling asleep on me? Frankfrankfrankfrankfrank! Now that you've heard the name of the love of your life, I've got you wide-awake, right? Now you can go to sleep. I'll see you in lunch tomorrow. Goodbye."

Erika hung the phone up and lay in the dark thinking about her room at the end of the hall at home. It was smaller than this one, and the bed was narrower, but it was better in every other way. It had a big window looking down on a little square of dirt and grass and some bushes. The walls the landlord said were green were really gray, but they were nicer than the faded blue walls at Dad's. The dresser had bigger drawers and a better mirror, the bed had a quilt instead of two old electric blankets with the wires taken out, and her stuffed dog Hilbert slept there seven nights a week. Plus she also had the advantage of being next to the kitchen and the bathroom, where the shower was better than Dad's and the hot water never seemed to run out. Her mom had given her the house key on a silver chain with a ruby-colored ball at each end.

"True or false," she whispered. "Mom needs me ten times more than Dad. No, twenty times."

She took a deep breath. She heard her father get up and pull the TV plug out of the wall to turn it off.

"True," she said. "But Dad needs a new TV a hundred times more than Mom, unless Bernie decides to take it away, which is why I need to be there. Case closed."

2

On a cold day a year ago, two of Jean's clients— sisters, twelve and fourteen—had been murdered by their father. Jean began the day by looking at a picture of them and remembering how sweet and smart they were, and how afraid.

At ten o'clock, she and the other two Children's Law Center lawyers, Rita Harris and Oswald Ingles, were sitting in Oz's office drinking coffee and discussing cases. They did it most Fridays. During the basketball season, they also discussed what was happening with the Boston Celtics. Jean's office was three times bigger than Oz's, with bigger chairs, a conference table to spread papers on, and windows overlooking the playground across the street, but his office was more fun to be in. Hanging on his door was a painting of a shark with big teeth and "Oz" written on its side, there were dozens of children's handprints in different colors all over the walls, and after the death last week of his pet goldfish, Mr. Justice, Oz had gotten a bigger bowl, with underwater plants to help keep the water clean, and a lady goldfish, Miss Mercy.

This morning Rita spoke first, asking advice about a seven-year-old client whose mother had fled with him to the Wharf Point Women's Shelter. "So now he's twenty miles away from his school, which is the one dependable thing in his life," she said. "How am I going to get him there on Monday?"

Oz went to his files and pulled out the phone number of a volunteer driver in Stony Creek, one town over from Wharf Point, who had helped him out two years before. "His grandson was a client two years ago, so he's always ready to do us a favor," he said.

Oz talked about a client named Annie, who had just found out that another kid in her class was her half brother. "It took us both by surprise," he said.

"How did Annie feel about it?" Rita asked.

"Fine," Oz said. "Her father doesn't want her mother to find out. Maybe she won't for a long time. Annie's whole life is keeping secrets from people. I'm surprised she told me. The kid's name is Scott, which is her favorite boy's name. It's his birthday next week, and she's in charge of cupcakes."

They began to talk about clients they knew who had to move all the time, one week going to Mom's place and the next to Dad's. Jean's idea was that the children should stay in one place and let their parents move every week. "It wasn't the kids who got the divorce," she'd say, "so why should they have to schlep back and forth all the time?"

"You just want to start a revolution," Oz said. "The parents would never stand for it."

"Right on both counts," Jean said. "Now, can I talk about my new client? I just got her yesterday, and I don't know much. Her name's Erika. Her mom brought her to court and Judge Gifford saw her and asked me to take her on. She's edgy. The court constable touched her elbow as they were going out the door yesterday and she jumped a mile. I'm going to have a hard time getting her to trust me, if she ever does." Jean looked at Rita. "She has eyes like yours, dark brown and a little bit sad."

Rita turned to Oz. "Do you think I have sad eyes?"

Oz shrugged his shoulders. "Don't ask me, I'm just a lawyer."

"She might never trust me," Jean said. "Not that she has any reason to so far. She knows exactly what she wants, to be living with her mother, starting right away. She makes fists on her lap when she tells you. We meet next Tuesday."

"That's all you know?" Rita asked.

"She's tall and beautiful. One other thing. She calls her mom's apartment, where she goes one night a week, *home*, and she calls her father's place, where she's been living for the last five years, *Dad's*." She stood up. "I've got some calls to make."

Jean went back to her office and dialed Mrs. Nevski's number. She let the phone ring twenty times and then dialed Pace Brothers' Ford and asked for Mr. Nevski in the body shop.

There was banging in the background. "Body shop."

"Hello, Mr. Nevski? This is Jean Rostow-Kaplan. Your daughter's attorney. I told you I'd be calling back? Do you have a minute now?"

"It's a bad time," he yelled.

"I'm sorry. Would it be better if I called you back after lunch?"

"I don't get lunch Fridays," he said. She heard a door slam. "Okay. I can talk for a minute. Why not? What do you want?"

"We need to set a time when we can get together," she said. "I'll be seeing Erika Tuesday, so any time after that would be fine."

"What do you need to know about her?" he asked. "Whatever it is, I can probably tell you right now on the phone."

"I need to know how you see things," Jean said.

"It's the bitch from start to finish," he said. "Erika knows. What'd she say about me yesterday?"

"We didn't talk about you. We talked about her."

"She didn't say anything about me?"

"She said you bake birthday cakes. You and I have the same goal, Mr. Nevski. We both want Erika happy. Getting together will help."

"That's what I want, her happy. Ask her. She'll tell you. We're going to court because of the bitch, nobody else."

Jean hated that word, but she was used to hearing it, and at least the man wasn't saying it in front of Erika.

He was quiet. She could hear the sounds of the body shop in the background. She waited.

"So," he said, "are we done? I know I wasn't there yesterday. I got a really busy life and Erika usually reminds me of stuff like that."

"She has a pretty busy life, too, Mr. Nevski."

"You think so? Between us, most kids don't know how good they got it. It's not their fault. How could they?"

"We still need to make an appointment," Jean said.

"Oh. Right. I'm pretty busy all week. The next couple weeks, too."

"How about Saturday, October twenty-ninth? Ten o'clock? Thirty Orchard Street. Do you know where that is?"

"I've lived here all my life," he said. "I guess I can find it. Sorry, I've got to go now." He hung up.

At four, after picking up Erika's records at the Grant Street Elementary School, Jean made a little detour and stopped her car across from Mrs. Nevski's apartment. As she was turning off the engine, somebody pulled down the shade on the third floor window. She got Erika's file out of her briefcase and dialed Mrs. Nevski's number. Nobody answered. She drove to the office and called Erika at her dad's.

"Hello."

"Hi, it's Jean."

"Hi."

"How are you?"

"Fine."

"Can you talk?"

"It's just me here," Erika said.

"I'll just take a minute," Jean said. "I was at Grant Street School today and they made me a copy of your file. Then I went by your mom's address. While I was sitting there, somebody pulled down the shades in the third-floor apartment, probably your mom or Karen. Anyone else live there?"

"It must have been one of them."

"I dialed their number before I left. Nobody answered."

Erika's voice got louder. "Sometimes Mom turns off the ringer so she can rest."

Jean nodded her head as if Erika could see. "That's probably it. I've got your fifth-grade report card in my hand. Mrs. Droste's class?"

"She was nice," Erika said.

"Good grades. There's a note with it where she says you saw a Doctor Gruenberg in October and November. Do you remember what it was about?"

"No," Erika said.

"It was around the time your mom and sister went to Arizona, so it was pretty busy. Nothing at all comes to mind?"

"Sorry," Erika said.

"No problem. You can't remember everything," Jean said. "Did I ask you about pictures of your family? Maybe Tuesday when you come in?"

"When I go home tomorrow," Erika said. "Mom's got two shoe boxes full from when we were rich. Not rich, exactly, but with money to go to the beach and do stuff."

"Great. Tryouts for the play on Monday?"

"I'm still not sure I'll do it," Erika said.

"Well, good luck if you do."

"Thanks."

Jean hung up and went down the hall to Kit's desk. "There's a Dr. Ann Gruenberg, a psychologist. Maybe she works for the school system, maybe she just consults. She's probably still in the area. Find out if she is. I need to ask her about a report she wrote."

Dear Diary,

I really like the scene on your cover. All kinds of things could come walking out of those woods. Bears. Skunks. An uncle you haven't seen since he pushed his wagon off a cliff. All kinds except a lawyer with her hand out saying, "Don't worry, just trust me." She might be really nice, but if I was out in the middle of the woods playing with my brother and my dog, I'd probably tell her to look for another client.

I'd like to live like that sometime.

Should I ask Sonia if Frank likes me Monday? Would I remember what she told me?

Yes. That I'd remember.

Jean didn't believe me. Not what I said about the doctor anyway, and not what I said about the phone. Would I have believed me? Probably, but then I believe everything people tell me.

The pizza in the cafeteria has tuna fish today? Sounds OK to me. The Stork's decided to do the play like it was a silent movie, just motions, no words? Great idea. The junior high's burned down so we're having classes in the courthouse? Terrific. A plastic surgeon's decided to fix Sonia's face for free? No. Nobody would say that unless it was true. Or they were evil.

You want to know two lies I'd like to believe? 1) Bernie's been arrested and sentenced to ten years, and 2) Karen's starting computer school Monday.

See, I'm not crazy, just too hopeful.

I'm starting to like you, no lie.

Love,

Erika

3

Saturday morning, just before she woke up, Erika had a nightmare. It began with her going to her mom's apartment to pick up her costumes for the play. When she got there the rooms were quiet, but she could feel that Bernie was somewhere. She looked in the hall closet, to make sure the costumes were there, and then went to her room to put down her backpack. When she turned around, Bernie was coming down the hall with a burning ball of newspaper in his hand. He smiled at her and threw the ball into the hall closet. Her costumes, which were soaked in gasoline to get them clean, burst into flames. He smiled at her again, said something, lit another newspaper ball, walked past her into her room, and set the bed on fire. She went down the hall to the front window in the living room and looked out at the street. There was yellow tape across the street at both ends, and some fire trucks parked pointing different ways, and there were firefighters and other people walking around laying out hoses, talking to each other, making little jokes and laughing and getting ready to put out a fire if they happened to find one somewhere. They were all nice people, and they knew what they were supposed to do, and they wanted to do it, but they didn't know where any fire might be. One of them looked up and smiled.

She waved her arms and tried to call out, but she couldn't make a sound, so she started going around to different rooms with fires in them, beating them out with a large hat, which was very good for the job. Each time she passed Bernie in the hall she would ask him to stop, but he would just look at her with his tiny eyes and say "sure sure sure," spitting at her through his bad teeth while lighting another ball of newspaper. She yelled at him please to stop so she could put out the last of the fires for when Mom and Karen came back, but he kept on and on and the smoke got worse and worse and she knew she was falling behind and soon the whole place would be full of fire and smoke and she would die and Mom would be left alone on the street with no place to go.

She woke up and looked at her clock. Seven. The buses started running at six. She got dressed, went in the kitchen, took out a box of cereal and the sugar and a bowl and spoon, and wrote a note.

Dear Daddy,

Here's your favorite! See you tomorrow!

Love,

Erika

She packed her books and took off for the bus stop. When she got to Ulster Street she ran down to number 1436 and up to the third floor, her heart beating fast, afraid that the apartment might have been burned out. She let herself in with her key and sniffed. There was nothing in the air except the usual blend of cigarette smoke and burned onions. She went down the hall to her room, laid her backpack in the corner, sat on the edge of the bed, and leaned forward, listening hard for Bernie's voice or Bernie's music. She didn't hear either.

She lay down, pulled the bedspread over herself, and laid Hilbert on her stomach.

She woke up at ten and went into the kitchen. Her mom was leaning over the table in her loose robe beating eggs in a bowl. "You're here. You must have tiptoed in. French toast?"

"Sure. Great."

"Just for you and Karen. Bernie's not here yet and I won't eat any. I'm going on a diet in honor of getting you back home. I'm really serious this time. Ask Karen."

She stopped beating the eggs, brought the bowl to the

table, and lit a cigarette. Erika hated to see her mom and Karen smoke, but she liked the sharp smell.

"I told Karen you'd be home by Thanksgiving. I had to tell her something. She was really upset. I hope you told your lawyer that's what you wanted."

"I said soon. She knows."

Her mom went to the cupboard, opened a jar of peanuts, and poured herself a handful. "Tell her Thanksgiving. It's good if people have something to aim at. So now everybody's lined up but your father. You just have to keep him from crying in front of the judge."

Karen came out of the bathroom with a towel wrapped around her head. She leaned against the door.

"I don't think he'll do that," Erika said.

"Yes he will, if he gets the chance. When you were little he cried twice as much as you did. You were the best-behaved child in the world. You did what you were told and never made a fuss. Everybody's going to be a lot happier when we get you home. He only wants to keep you so I can't have you."

"My lawyer says she needs to come visit sometime," Erika said.

Her mother smiled, got four slices of bread out of the freezer, and put them in the toaster to defrost.

"Bring her on. We'll be ready. We'll invite her to come for Thanksgiving dinner. We'll do turkey, stuffing, two kinds of potatoes, everything."

"She's got a husband and at least one kid," Erika said.

Her mom looked at Karen. "How did we cook it last year? Did we do stuffing?"

"You wanted ham."

"No. Ham? No. Really?"

Karen took the towel off her head and began combing out her hair, spraying little droplets of water on the table. She looked down at Erika. "I didn't hear you come in."

"I didn't want to wake people up."

Her mom opened the refrigerator, took out butter and syrup, and put them on the table in front of Karen. "Ham. That's original. Creative."

"You said you wanted something different for a change," Karen said. "Then you wouldn't eat it because you said it tasted like one of those wild pigs they have out there."

"Right. Now I remember. I helped cook. I remember peeling the potatoes."

"You didn't peel one potato."

"Yes I did."

"No you didn't."

"That was way back in the past," Erika said. "Everybody knows Phoenix potatoes are part cactus, which makes them ten times harder to peel."

Her mom smiled. "You learn something new every day. Anyway, this year I'm cooking everything and we're going to invite everybody's lawyers and everybody's lawyers' families. They have to work together." She looked at Erika. "You didn't meet Attorney Klecko, but I told him all about you. He wants to meet you. He told me so."

Erika went and got out some dishes. "When I saw him and you in front of the courthouse, he was waving his arms and yelling at you."

Her mom took a puff on her cigarette, put it down, and came over to kiss Erika on the back of the neck. "Don't be upset. He's a nice man and he's going to help get you home. He wasn't yelling. Karen was there all the time. She knows." She looked at Karen. "He didn't yell, did he?"

Karen combed harder. "I don't know. I went to get Bernie so we could go home."

"He was waving because he was saying goodbye," her mom said. "But talking about Bernie's car reminds me. For a brand-new car it's not so smooth. And it pulls to the right every time he puts his foot on the brake."

"No it doesn't," Karen said.

"Yes it does, but I'm not going to let it bother me. So, Erika, what are we going to have for dinner? I don't have an appetite, so you can put anything on the table, and Bernie and Karen are going to be out at a party or something. Anything you want is fine as far as I'm concerned, but I think you should cook something really good. The Stop & Shop's right around the corner, so there's no way you can say it's too much trouble to get the ingredients. Let's talk about something else. I'm supposed to see your lawyer. It must feel funny being only fourteen, well, almost fifteen, and having a lawyer. Are you okay with it?"

She gave Erika two slices of French toast, then dropped two more in the frying pan. "We're almost out of syrup, by the way, when you shop. I have nothing in the world against women lawyers, but if it came to talking to a jury, I'd pick a man to do it every time. The men would look up to him, and the women he could sweet-talk."

"I don't think there is a jury. It's just the judge."

"He might not like having a woman telling him what to do, but he picked her, so he probably likes her. I don't want her coming here and poking around. I hate anybody to see this place. If we had more money I'd be able to put it in shape. Every room in the place cries out for paint. Plus the hall. Your room first of all, Erika. I got Bernie to bring me some books of colors from the paint store we can look at. They're in the living room. Of course we don't want to talk about moving until your lawyer comes and goes. We'll have to make sure she comes on a Sunday, so we can neaten the place up Saturday."

"I think she wants it to be a surprise," Erika said, knowing Jean wouldn't be fooled. Then she heard a key in the lock and Bernie's footsteps in the hall. He came to the kitchen door holding up a paper bag in one stumpy hand and pushing his key ring deep into his pocket with the other.

The worst thing about Bernie coming Saturday morning was that Erika's mom wasn't always completely dressed when he got there. Not that she was ever undressed, but sometimes she'd have her robe loose and she'd be leaning over doing something and he'd stare at her. He was staring at her now, so Erika took the fork out of her hand and told her to sit down and lean back and relax.

Bernie smiled through his rotten teeth. "You can all eat later. Follow me to the living room," he said. "Come sit on the couch and take a look at the pictures of my baby." Karen grabbed Erika's arm and pulled her down the hall after him. Bernie was already sitting in the middle of the couch. He slapped the cushions. "Erika right and you left," he said to Karen. "Becky, you look over my shoulder. You got to see these pictures. Talk about beautiful. I already bought the frame. Gold."

His baby, Claudia, was fourteen months old, a great kid, lots of fun to play with, so Erika really wanted to look at the pictures. Bernie went through them fast. Erika's mom came in and stood leaning over them. In the last three pictures, Claudia was sitting on the mother's lap. The mother looked ten years older than Karen, but her hair was nice and she had a nice smile. So how did a man like Bernie get a nice woman like that to go with him? Just his aftershave should have made people sick enough to stay miles away. It smelled like the soap over the sinks in the girls' bathrooms at school, except stronger.

Suddenly he slammed the book shut, grabbed Erika's knee and squeezed until it hurt, jumped up, and put the pictures back in the paper bag. "We got to go," he said, pushing Karen out the door ahead of him.

Erika's mom went back in the kitchen and ate the last two pieces of French toast, and then they watched cartoons on the flat-screen TV Bernie had given them. During one of the commercials her mom said, "You think you'll be able to remember everything? You know, like your speeches in the play if you get it? All the lines you'll have to remember and what you're supposed to do? I don't want you to be in something that's going to get in the way of our case in court."

"I don't go to court," Erika said. "I'm not allowed. That's why they gave me a lawyer. As far as the play goes, I'm not even sure I'm going to try out, and even if I do I might not get the part, so we probably won't have to worry about it."

Her mom shook her head and turned off the TV. "You'll get it. But who wants to talk about that when we can talk about painting your room the exact right color?" She reached under the end table and took out a paint company color book. There were thousands of colors to choose from. Erika wanted bright yellow, and after going to the window to see how they looked in daylight, she picked one out.

The rest of the morning they hung out. In the afternoon they took the bus to the mall and ate pizza and bought a lamp.

Dear Diary,

It's Saturday night, and I'm in my room at home that's going to be painted "Sunny Umbrella." Do you like the name? I do.

I'm going to tell you something nobody knows, which I never even told Carrie. At the end of dress rehearsal for Bye Bye Birdie *last year, I was still up on the platform where we threw confetti for the last scene and the Stork came on the stage and started going over what different people still had to work on for opening night. Frank came and stood right under me and he held on to my right ankle like it was some resting place and kept holding it the whole time the Stork was talking. Then afterward he didn't pay any attention to me at all, like he didn't think I'd remember it, or like* he *didn't remember it, but some things you never forget.*

I know *he knew it was an ankle and whose it was.*

If I get to play Kate, Frank could play John, the soldier she's engaged to. It probably won't happen.

I just heard Karen and Bernie come in, so I'm going to put you under Hilbert and turn off the light now.

Good night.

Love,

Erika

P.S. I've got to remember to get a family picture for Jean. Maybe from the beach when I was a baby and everybody was happy.

4

Sunday night, Erika and her dad went to Angelo's Restaurant for dinner. At the end of the meal he pushed back his plate and asked her what her mom had said about him.

"Nothing much," Erika said.

"Why not?"

"I don't know."

"So the bitch didn't say anything, just ate what you cooked? Did she ask you about your lawyer? She's the reason you got one. What's the woman's name again?"

"Jean Rostow-Kaplan."

"I'm going to see her in her office. You'll have to remind me when the time comes. If I wasn't so busy at work, I'd go sooner and beat your mother to it. Maybe I'll call Rostow-

Kaplan tonight and get it changed to earlier. You got her cell phone number, right? What is it?"

"She told me not to give it out. Maybe you can call her at her office tomorrow."

Her dad balled up his napkin and threw it on the table so it bounced and hit the back of the booth. "Her home number's got to be in the phone book. I'm not going to let the bitch tell her side of the story first."

"You could call there tonight and leave a message," Erika said.

He shook his head. "Just because I don't have a lawyer and I wasn't in court that one time doesn't mean I can't do what I want or take care of my child. I can call her house and talk to her. I'm not saying I will, but I'm thinking about it."

As soon as they got home, Erika looked up the law center number in the phone book and gave it to him, but he grabbed the book from her, looked up Jean's home number, dialed it, talked to her for a minute, and then hung up.

He grinned at Erika. "Well, in case you want to know, she's got three kids. She just told me. Right now she's busy with her son Nathan on some school report he's writing. On Brazil. Or some country like that. She's going to call me back in a minute. Maybe she will, maybe she won't. If she doesn't in ten minutes by the clock, I'll just call her again. Or not, depending on how I feel."

The Brazil report took Jean more time than she'd expected, so she didn't dial Mr. Nevski's number until almost nine. He answered right away.

"Before we start," she said, "I need to remind you that, as Erika's lawyer, I can't discuss any element of the case without her permission."

"You want to talk to her?"

"No, thank you."

"You don't have to worry about me asking you the wrong questions, because she's right here next to me making faces."

"What did you call me at home for, Mr. Nevski?"

"I want us to have a friendly talk before the bitch tells her lies."

"I see. Is Erika still next to you?"

"You can talk to her if you want."

"No. I need to make something clear to you before we say goodbye. You are never, sir, not ever, to call Mrs. Nevski a bitch in front of my client. Do you know what a bitch is?"

"I just called you to have a friendly talk."

"And I do not mean to be unfriendly. I am merely asking you a question. Do you know what a bitch is?"

"Sure. I used to hunt with my father. It's a dog."

"That means you know what a son of a bitch is."

"Sure."

"And also a daughter of a bitch. Now I ask you, do you

wish to encourage my client to think of herself in those terms?"

"That's stupid. She wouldn't think like that."

"Nobody has any way of knowing what Erika will think or feel about anything, Mr. Nevski. But let me tell you this. If I discover that you have used that word in front of her to describe her mother even one time, I will feel free to ask her permission to inform Judge Gifford that you have done so in spite of my clear instructions. I assure you, sir, he will not be pleased. Do we understand one another?"

"Yes."

"Good. Now, did you want to make an appointment in my office earlier than October twenty-ninth?"

"No."

"Then I'll say good night."

Erika's dad brushed past her. His face was sweating. She followed him into the kitchen.

He opened the refrigerator door. "Why did I take the trouble to talk to her?" he said. "I was ready to take off work and go see her this week, but now she can wait. I'm trying to be friendly and she gives me this cross-examination. I don't think she really wants to see me. I think she was trying to get rid of me."

"No, Daddy, I'm sure she wasn't."

"How do you know?"

"She wants to be fair to everybody."

He looked into the refrigerator again. "You talked to her for five minutes in her car and all of a sudden you know what she wants? Lucky you. I'm not going to think about it. I don't care." He bent over. "I bought a six-pack yesterday and I only drank two. Where's the rest?"

She went to the refrigerator and stood beside him. The other four cans, in their plastic holder, were on the top shelf next to the orange juice. She twisted one out, gave it to him, and closed the refrigerator door.

He sat down at the table. "You know I don't mean it when I call your mother a bitch. I mean I *do* mean it, but I don't mean anything about you. It doesn't bother you, right?"

She didn't know what to say. When she was little, he and her mom used to say they were going to kill each other, so bad-mouthing each other from a distance didn't seem much at all. The only word that still bothered her was Mom's name for him, Crybaby.

He popped the top of the can. "You say *bitch*. I heard you say it last week about some teacher on the phone with Carrie. Everybody says it. It's just a word. According to your lawyer, if she finds out I said it where you could hear, she's going to tell the judge and put me in the wrong with him." He got up and went to the refrigerator again. "You want some orange juice or something?"

"No, thanks."

He let the door slam shut and came back to the table. "You wouldn't tell on me if it slipped out, would you?"

"No."

"Promise?"

"Promise."

He slid the can around in wet circles on the table.

Erika went to the refrigerator, almost tiptoeing, and took out a Pepsi. When she looked back at her dad, he was crying and waving his hands in front of his face. "You know it isn't anything about you," he said. "You know I wouldn't call you anything but Erika or baby."

She went over to him and kissed him on top of the head. "I know," she said. "Really, it's okay. And if you say it by mistake, I won't tell."

He leaned back, grabbed a paper napkin, and blew his nose. "Not because of her, but if you don't want me to say it in front of you anymore, I won't."

Erika nodded her head. "It might be better."

"We could make a deal and neither of us use it. Do you think? She talked to me like I was a kid. I'm not a kid. I've got a job. I've got a child."

Dear Diary,

I think there's a God of Cable, and when He finds out that you've been tapping into the line without paying, He makes all the programs stupid, and if you don't notice they're stupid He begins to fool around with the volume knob so you have to get up and down all the time.

Bernie pays Mom's bill, so the Cable God leaves him alone.

Daddy just came in and told me he wants me to tell Jean he hasn't used the word since we talked. It's only been an hour but it's a start.

Love,

Erika

She put the diary back in her suitcase, opened her algebra book, and took out the two pages the Stork had told her he wanted her to try out with. She had to come onstage, pick up a sandwich, take a bite, and tell her father what a terrible man their lawyer is. She wondered if the Stork would hand her a peanut butter sandwich and tell her to chew on it while she was saying the lines. He might do something like that. You never knew with him.

There was one line at the end of the second page she knew not even a real actress could make sound right.

But don't fool yourself about him, Father, for all that. The man is a fish, a hard, cold-blooded, supercilious, sneering fish.

Even if she said it exactly the right way, however that would be, everybody in the auditorium would laugh. If the Stork gave her a sandwich and she came to that line, she would at least wait to say it until after she'd swallowed.

She turned off the light and whispered the line five times into the dark, and then she began to laugh. Maybe the best thing for her would be to be sick tomorrow.

5

When Erika woke up she did feel a little bit sick, but she went to school anyway.

In algebra she got back her test. It was an 84. All her answers were right, but Mrs. Meigs took points off two questions for having the method wrong. Next to the longest one she wrote, *Why so many steps?* The social studies quiz didn't come back. Maybe it never would. She didn't care, at least not much.

Lunch period she told Carrie she really should try out.

"No chance," Carrie said. "You do it, go ahead, it won't make any difference to me."

"I probably won't."

"Sure you will, but it's a completely dumb play. I went into the Stork's office and stole a copy Friday hoping it would be good, but it isn't. Everybody who comes is going to laugh at it or fall asleep. *Nothing* interesting happens. Nothing. And Kate, the part the Stork wants for you? It's got three hundred and twenty-eight lines. I counted. You ever notice that Frank's shorter than you? He kisses you twice. You're going to have to bend over. The audience is going to love that."

"We're the same height."

"When you're standing in a hole."

"I'll wear flat shoes."

"If the Stork lets you. He might want you to have to stoop."

Erika looked across the cafeteria. Frank was at the far corner table with a bunch of guys, gearheads, mostly. Sonia Merrero was sitting across from him. She was in love with him, too.

"You know what the Stork does for tryouts? He gets you up onstage with all the lights on so you can't see anybody out in the seats. There's just his voice, like the voice of God telling you to do this and do that. Did you know that?"

She did. She had sat in the last row of the auditorium last April watching Frank try out for *Bye Bye Birdie*. "Maybe it's better not to be able to see who's watching," she said.

"Three hundred and twenty-eight lines! Sonia'll play the maid. You know how her face is all screwed up after that car accident, so she has one eye higher than the other? Five or six times you're going to have to look at her and ask for something. So, how will you decide which eye to look in, the high one or the low one? You could take turns, left eye, right eye, so she doesn't think you're playing favorites."

All Monday afternoon, right up through P.E., Erika thought she probably wouldn't try out, but when they started calling the buses she thought about Frank and how nice Sonia was and how when you're in a play you get to be in this whole different world every day for six weeks, so she went to the auditorium.

It was just the way it had been last year. The twelve kids who were trying out sat in front. The Stork had all the stage lights turned on and the auditorium lights turned off. He called Erika first, and sent Frank up onstage with her to read the lines for Kate's father. Every few lines the Stork would yell in his sharp voice, "Louder! We can't hear you!" After less than a page he yelled, "Do those first three lines again!" and after she did them three times he yelled, "Okay. Next!" so she never got to do the supercilious fish line. She was glad, but she was a little sorry, too, because it was the only one she knew by heart.

Frank said, "You were great," as she passed him on the way off the stage, but she knew he was lying. He had already gotten his hair cut short for the soldier's part, shorter probably than the Stork wanted it. She walked up the aisle to the last row to hear him read his lines. It was the scene at the beginning where he goes to see Kate's father to ask for permission to marry her. He stood stiff, with his chin back, but he was supposed to be a soldier and Erika thought he did it just right. She could hear every word he said even standing under the balcony. He acted like it was nothing for him to be on the stage.

On the way to her locker she passed the Stork's office door. Before lunch Wednesday the cast list would be taped on the glass. No use thinking about it. The next big thing was tomorrow, seeing her lawyer.

6

Jean walked into the Grant Street School Tuesday morning early and the principal took her to Mrs. Droste's classroom. The teacher was sitting at her desk examining an asthma inhaler. She had gray hair, cut very short, and a blue suit with a pleated skirt fifteen or twenty years out of date. The principal introduced them. "It's about Erika Nevski," he said.

Mrs. Droste put the inhaler in her middle desk drawer and locked it. "She's the kind of girl who makes fifth grade a pleasure," she said. "How is she?"

"She seems very well," Jean said. "I haven't spent much time with her so far. I'll see her for the second time later today."

Mrs. Droste smiled. "Tell her hello for me."

"I will," Jean said.

She turned her head and looked at the principal, waiting for him to leave. He did.

"Without going into detail," she said, "I can tell you Erika's the object in a custody case. In order to get a sense of her past, I'd like to know how she was when she was in your fifth grade. That was the year her mother left the state. I know only that there were two months, October and November, when she wasn't at her best."

"That's right." Mrs. Droste reached down to her bottom drawer and went through a pile of class photographs, pulled one out, and laid it on the desk. It showed three rows of ten- and eleven-year-olds.

Jean spotted Erika right away, the tall girl with short hair in the back row. "She has long hair now," she said.

"It was long when she started fifth grade," Mrs. Droste said. "Then one day at the end of September she stayed inside during recess and cut off most of it in the girls' room. She tried to flush it down the toilet, thinking if she got rid of it I wouldn't notice it was missing. Of course the toilet ran over. It was very embarrassing for her. That night her father tried to fix her hair by cutting it evenly, and made it look worse. So he took her to a hairdresser who cut it to look as if it was short on purpose. Beautiful hair. Some red in it."

"Did she say why she'd done it?"

"I didn't ask," Mrs. Droste said. "There seemed to be a whole cascade of bad things going on with her, so butchering her hair was nothing. She had already reverted to writing in big letters, like a first grader. She couldn't do simple arithmetic. You'd ask her five take away two and she'd get a look of panic in her eyes. It scared all the other kids, and you know when kids get scared they can get cruel. Mostly they just stayed away from her."

Mrs. Droste pointed to the girl sitting right below Erika. "All but her. Carrie Ives. Carrie stuck with her, defended her, even tried to do her work for her. One day a girl laughed at the way Erika was holding her pencil and Carrie hit her on the head with a stapler. I sent Erika to a psychologist, Ann Gruenberg, who is the best of the best. In two months Erika was back doing grade-level work again, and by spring she was scoring near the top of the class."

"What did Dr. Gruenberg do?"

"She played games with her, took her places, did craft projects. Erika's mom had left the home. Dr. Gruenberg got Erika to write letters to her. Went to the post office and picked out love stamps and flower stamps, got her making pot holders to send. They were very well made. She gave me one I still use."

Erika got to Orchard Street five minutes early and went inside the old building, but then she walked past the Children's Law Center door twice, thinking it was a preschool because the floor of the reception area was full of toys. When she went in, she had to step around a little girl about three years old. A man she guessed was the girl's father was sitting on a chair behind her. The woman at the desk got up and shook her hand. She was about twenty and wearing a blouse with pictures of fire engines all over it. "I'm Kit. Ms. Rostow-Kaplan is in with a client now, but she'll be with you soon. The girl working with our worn-out blocks is Jade."

Erika took off her backpack, sat down on the floor next to Jade, and began trying to find blocks flat enough to build a tower with.

After watching them a few minutes, Jade's father reached down, grabbed one of Jade's braids, and pulled off the little plastic barrette holding the end of it. "Look what you've done," he said. "It's coming all loose." Jade pulled away and started screaming. Kit turned away from her desk and asked Jade if she'd like to help her do some work on the copy machine. "As soon as her hair's fixed," her father said and leaned down in his chair and started slapping at Jade's head, pretending he was trying to get it neat. Jade kept screaming. Erika grabbed the brush out of her backpack, pulled Jade toward her so she was out of her father's reach, picked up the loose barrette, and started brushing her hair out. Then, without looking at Jade's father, Erika laid her brush on the floor and redid the little girl's braids.

When she was finished, Jade picked up the brush and said, "My turn," but her father grabbed her and pulled her onto his lap.

"Leave this nice girl alone, you've played with her enough," he said.

He began to tickle her.

Erika hated forced tickling. Two weeks ago when she was home, Bernie had sneaked up behind her and tried to tickle her in the ribs. She had spun around, hitting him and cutting his cheek with one of her bracelets. She was glad she had hurt him, and he knew it.

Now Jade was out of breath and begging her father to stop. Erika turned away and stowed her brush in her back-pack.

Kit suddenly stood up. "Copy machine time," she said. "The machine needs to grind it out. Can't wait any longer."

The father stopped, and Kit picked Jade off his lap and carried her into the big walk-in safe where the copier was. Pretty soon it was spitting out paper.

To stay busy and avoid looking at the father, Erika kept working on the block tower, letting it fall down and building it up again. She heard Jean coming down the hall talking with somebody about children and parents having written contracts about doing chores around the house. A few seconds later, Jean walked into the waiting room with a girl with the same tiny eyes as Jade's father. Instead of her black courtroom suit, Jean was wearing dungarees and a sweatshirt with a Boston Celtics logo on the front. The father stood up, Kit carried Jade out of the safe, and the three of them went away.

Jean led Erika down the hall to her office, passing two empty offices on the way. On the desk in the second one was a huge goldfish bowl.

Jean sat behind her desk, and Erika sat on the chair next to it. "The building used to be a shoe factory," Jean said. "This was the payroll manager's office. There's a walk-in safe in the reception room, where we have the copier. Plus toys and picture books to give little kids to take home. In the old days they'd get cash from the bank Thursday afternoons, put it in envelopes that night, and pay it out Fridays. They were robbed twice. Different robbers a week apart. Good news gets around."

"What did they do?"

"The managers? They decided to pay the workers in the morning, which for some reason ended the crime wave." She turned a framed picture in Erika's direction. "This is my husband, Brian; Nathan, our oldest; and Martin and Christa."

Erika blushed and hit her knee with her fist. "I'm sorry," she said. "I forgot to bring in a picture."

Jean smiled. "No problem. Next time. Did you try out for the play?"

"I wasn't any good at all."

"I think you were probably very good," Jean said. "I haven't seen you act, but I've seen you walk, so I know how you might look to an audience."

"When did you watch me walking?"

"Last week, in the parking lot. You walked away from me,

then you turned around and walked back to me, then you walked away again."

"How do I walk?"

"In as straight a line as possible. Have you got any questions about what I told you in the car? Or anything you're wondering about?"

If I don't ask questions, Erika thought, she's going to.

"Well, there are some things."

"Like what?"

Erika made up some questions about the law. What were the differences between different courts? Were there cases where you had to have juries? When was it better to have a judge decide? What did you need to do to appeal a verdict? Did somebody have to take special courses in law school to do children's law? Did any of her children ever say they wanted to become lawyers?

When it got to be five and she figured the session was almost over, Erika asked the only important question she had. "Would it go faster if my father had a lawyer?"

"It might and it might not," Jean said. "It would depend on the kind of lawyer he had. Some lawyers become lawyers because they love to fight. They make long lists of everything their clients could possibly want, and then add some extras, and try to get it all. Other lawyers want to find a solution that's more or less fair to everybody, so they try to work things out. Did your dad ask you to ask me about it?"

"No. I'd just like to speed things up."

Jean got a piece of paper out of her top drawer and wrote down two numbers. "The first one is the Legal Aid number," she said. "He might not fit their guidelines, but their lawyers don't charge a fee. The second would provide him with a list of possibilities."

"I don't want it to keep on going and going forever," Erika said.

Jean smiled at her. "Neither do I, but I need to know more about you before I can represent you in front of Judge Gifford. That's why I went to see Mrs. Droste. She told me to tell you hello, by the way. You still don't remember seeing a Dr. Ann Gruenberg?"

Erika felt ashamed. "Are you sure it was me?" she said.

Jean handed her the record. "Mrs. Droste mentions it at the bottom of the page, where it says 'Additional Comments.' There's her name, Ann Gruenberg. Nothing comes to mind? She would have gotten you to talk about your family. She might have asked you to draw some pictures for her, maybe shown you drawings of a family and asked you to guess who the people were and what they were doing. No memory?"

Erika shook her head. "I'm sorry."

"Don't worry about it. Kit found her address. She's still living in the city. If I can get a copy of her report, I'll let you know what it says." She sat back. "What do you want? Not what do you want out of this case, but what do you want out of life?"

Erika looked around the room. "For everybody to be happy, I guess."

"Mom? Dad? Karen?"

"Sure. And the people I babysit for. The kids in the play. Everybody."

"Including you?"

"I guess I'm like everybody else."

"Some people can only be happy when they're miserable, or making other people miserable."

"That's not me," Erika said.

Jean smiled. "I didn't think so." She stood. "It's my night to cook dinner," she said. "Let me know whether you get a part in the play."

In bed, Erika kept remembering Jade. At midnight, she got up and dialed Jean's cell phone number.

"Hello?"

"Jean? It's Erika. I'm sorry to call you so late. I'll only take a minute. It's probably nothing."

"Take your time."

"It's about today. While I was at the office? Jade's daddy started slapping her on the head. He didn't do it all that hard, but it just makes me wonder, if he does it where people can see, what does he do when nobody's around?"

"Thanks. Calling me was the right thing to do. Ask me to tell you my Bobby Kennedy story next time we see each other."

"What is it?"

"It's pretty short. I'll tell you now. Bobby Kennedy was a senator from New York. Early one morning he was out walking his dog on Park Avenue, and while he was standing waiting for the light to turn green he saw this little kid, maybe eight or nine, with a cigarette in his mouth, and he stopped him and told him that smoking cost too much money and was bad for his health, and the kid said, 'What business is it of yours?' and walked away, and when Kennedy got home he said to his wife, 'It's everybody's business when children get hurt.' That's the story."

"Is that why you became a children's lawyer?"

"As a matter of fact, yes."

7

Wednesday morning, Jean looked into Oz's office. "My new client, Erika, called last night, after Brian and I were in bed," she said.

"What about?" he asked.

"Jade. The girl who poured Pepsi in your first fishbowl. Clarissa's little sister. Erika didn't want to bother me, and she got off the phone as fast as she could."

"With the sausage pigtails."

"Right. Erika was worried about the way the father handled Jade. I wonder how much sleep she gets worrying about people."

"Is he a danger to his children?"

"I don't know. Kit was working late yesterday and said

something to me as I was going out the door. She didn't see him slapping her, but she told me he was doing some pretty aggressive tickling. He could be one of these parents who terrify their children and tell themselves they want it. Clarissa loves him, but I know she's terrified of him. I need to get some psychological tests done on the man. I should have done it before. And I'll ask Minerva Haddad in the clerk's office to look up the domestic assault charge against him last year. His wife dropped it, but I want to know exactly what her original complaint was."

"He won't like being tested."

Jean shook her head. "No. He'll love it. He thinks he's the world's most perfect father. If he does refuse, I may recommend that he not have any unsupervised visits with either child. Kit's got good judgment, and now Erika's saying the same thing, and I trust Erika."

On the way back to homeroom after seventh period, Erika passed Frank in the hall. He kept looking in the other direction, and she was sure he had seen the cast list and her name wasn't on it. She decided Carrie had been right to tell her not to do it. Of course she could still be on the stage crew, but that wasn't the same thing as playing Kate and being kissed by him twice.

As Erika was putting stuff in her backpack and listening to the bus numbers being called, Sonia came over with a big smile on her messed-up face. "You're going to be terrific," she said.

Then Erika knew.

"You got the part," Sonia said. "You're Kate."

Erika zipped up her backpack and put it on.

"You didn't look at the list?" Sonia asked.

"I guess not."

"Frank's playing John. He read with you, right?"

"He read the father's part."

"This is better."

Erika remembered his hand around her ankle. "I saw him in the hall. He didn't say anything. He didn't even look at me. Maybe he didn't see me."

Sonia shrugged her shoulders. "He's shy, except when he's onstage. The first meeting's in the band room tomorrow. It's in big red letters on the bottom of the cast list. The Stork calls it a rehearsal, but it's really just him and Mrs. Fine talking. He'll wait awhile to start yelling."

Sonia's bus was called, and she started to leave.

"Who's he making you?" Erika asked, even though she was sure she knew.

"The maid. It's a great part. She does some funny stuff, and everybody loves her."

"You want to trade? You've been in every play since sixth grade. You should be Kate."

Sonia shook her head slowly. With her nose pushed flat and her eyes out of line, the Stork wasn't going to let her be the love interest. It was wrong, but it was so, and they both knew it. "I'm satisfied," she said.

The first thing Erika did when she got back to her father's was dial home and hang up after two rings. That was her and her mom's private system, two rings, call me back at Dad's, three rings, call me at Carrie's. Of course, it only worked when the ringer was on.

The phone rang. "Mom?"

"You got the part?"

"Yes."

"Is Carrie in it, too?"

"She decided not to try out."

"Then your friendship's over."

Erika's heart stopped for a second. Her mom made a lot of mistakes, but when she made a prediction, it always came true. "No it's not," she said. "We'll always be best friends."

Her mom put on her singsong voice. "If you say so. You're going to be wonderful. That's what moms are always supposed to think when their daughters get big parts in plays, even when they're only school plays. What are you going to wear?"

"I don't know. It's supposed to be a hundred years ago in England."

"I'll sew all your dresses. I'll call the school and tell them not to worry about it. Who's in charge of the costumes?"

"Mrs. Fine, I guess. Probably. She always is."

"I'll call her. You and I can go shopping for patterns and material Saturday when you're home. Hold on, Bernie's in the living room. I want to go tell him. He's going to be so happy. You don't give him credit for how much he's in your corner. You could start now being a little nicer to him. You know he's still got a scar on his cheek from when you hit him that time. I'll get him. Wait."

The phone banged down.

Erika waited, and then Bernie picked up.

"Erika? Your mom tells me you got a part in the school play. That's great. I thought about being an actor once."

She said nothing.

"What's your lawyer think now that she's working for a star?"

"I don't know."

"It's none of my business, but personally I'd never trust a lawyer who came free. You still listening?"

"Yes."

"If she was any good she'd be out on her own, with her own office, a real practice. You always want to have people around you who you pay yourself so they know they've got to do what you tell them. Free lawyers are there for an easy paycheck every week. She lets you down, all you need is to ask me and I'll get you a better one and pay for him with my own money. Let's face it, the only people in the world who really love you are the people who love you, you know what I mean? I have some tricks I could tell you about memorizing lines. We used to call it memorization when I was in school. They still do that?"

Erika moved the phone from her right ear to her left ear and rubbed her right ear against her shoulder. "I have to call somebody else now," she said.

"Okay. No problem. Here's your mom back."

"Erika? You've got to think about your complexion now, so keep your face scrubbed and stay away from chocolate."

"Okay, Mom. I have to go now. Goodbye."

"Goodbye. See you soon."

Erika hung up and went into the bathroom, examined her forehead in the mirror, and washed her face. The phone rang again. It was Carrie's mom. "I hear congratulations are in order," Mrs. Ives said. "You're going to be wonderful. I want to help you. I can drive you to your dad's after rehearsals."

"Daddy lives pretty near," Erika said.

"How about the days rehearsals run late? And it's fall, so every day it gets darker earlier. And you need to get home and make your dad's dinner and do your homework and study your lines and still get your beauty rest. Besides, you're my adopted daughter. Sometimes I think we understand each other better than Carrie and I do."

Erika said a ride would be nice once in a while and thanked her. Then Carrie came on.

"I already warned you, didn't I? The play's really stupid. Also I counted your lines. Three hundred and twenty-eight. I got to go now. Call me later."

Erika went into the living room and flopped on the couch. Their old black-and-white portable television was sitting on top of the television with the bad volume control. She shook her head. Dad must have gone down to the basement before he went to work and gotten it out. It was so old it didn't even have a remote. She banged a sofa cushion and watched the dust fly and thought about being poor. Last year in social studies they had spent two weeks on the Great Depression, when almost everybody was out of work and standing in line at soup kitchens. But some of the rich stayed rich through it all and kept on buying whatever they wanted but at lower prices. In America everybody was supposed to look at everybody else the same way, but only people who were rich or dumb thought anybody did. If you had money you could get away with stuff. When Carrie stole her neighbor's car last year and knocked down the lady's baby crab apple tree, they just bought her a new tree, plus some special kind of magnolia for her back yard, and everybody was happy.

She hated it when Carrie went along with her to the Salvation Army store. For one thing, Carrie always found better stuff. And every time she bought a shirt or a skirt or a pair of jeans, even if it fit her perfectly and looked like it had never been worn, she did it for *fun* and she never, ever wore it. It was completely different with Erika. She bought stuff to wear every day, and it wasn't *fun*, it was just what she had to do.

When the kids were all together in the band room Thursday afternoon, the Stork stood up on the conductor's podium with the script in his hand and made a speech. He was a tall man with a short beard, and when he looked at you he would sometimes make his pale blue eyes very big.

"At five minutes to eight on Thursday, November seventeenth, thirty-five and a half days from now, you will be onstage in the auditorium, made up, in costume, ready for the curtain to go up on the first act of *The Winslow Boy* by Terence Rattigan. Those days will go by very fast, so the time to get serious is right now."

He put on his wide-eyed look and scanned the room.

"I heard somebody at the tryouts say our play was dull.

She is not among us today. It's a great show, and each one of you is going to be great in it. It's not a musical. It's not a Saturday morning cartoon. It doesn't take place on a spaceship, or in the jungle, or in a jail, or on a bus wired with explosives. Boring, right? No. Wrong." He tapped his head, and then his heart. "Everything that happens in this play happens here and here. What you think and feel, the audience will think and feel. If you've got your heads and hearts somewhere else, they'll tune you out. If you put your heads and hearts in the play, they'll be your slaves."

He took a deep breath and tried to smile. "Putting on a play is not an exercise in democracy. There's one boss. Shall I tell you who that boss is? I don't think I need to. I tell you to do something, and you do it. Maybe it feels funny. Maybe it *is* funny. Maybe people laugh at you. Maybe you have an idea of how you could do it better, but your job right then is to move the way I want you to move, and say your lines the way I want you to say them. Clear? Afterward, maybe, if you want to, you come to my office and tell me politely what your better idea is. I'll listen. I may even accept it. Or better yet, write me a letter and put it in my box in the office."

He looked directly at Erika. "I had the tryouts in the auditorium because I wanted to know right away how each one of you would look and sound onstage. Erika looked fine. She could give you all standing straight lessons. But she's going to have to work on her voice volume. We will all teach each other many things. Thanks to Miss Worley, rehearsals will take place right here in the band room for the time being. When you get onstage in the auditorium, you'll start to work on being your characters for an audience. Here for the next two weeks, you will work on being your characters for yourselves and for each other. You are the Winslows.

"From today on, Erika, you will think about nothing else but being Kate, and Bobby will think about nothing but being your father, and Sonia will think about being your servant, and Josh will think about being your little brother Ronnie. And so on. Get the idea? Erika, I'm asking you, do you get the idea?"

Erika grabbed her script tighter. "Yes."

"You live in a big house in London. It's 1910. Queen Victoria has been dead less than ten years. All of you except Ronnie remember her funeral and how sad it made you. You live in the richest, most powerful city in the richest, most powerful country in the world. I want you to know it in your souls.

"As far as this room that Miss Worley is *very kindly* loaning to us goes, the first ones to arrive every day will fold up the chairs and the music stands, push those risers back into the corner, and put away this podium I'm standing on. After rehearsal those who didn't help at the start will move things back where they belong before they go.

"Learn your lines, learn your lines, learn your lines. Now Mrs. Fine is going to talk to you about costumes and props."

Mrs. Fine, who was very young but had snow white hair,

stayed in her seat and talked for about two minutes about English clothing a hundred years ago. She would be giving all the actors lists of props they were responsible for. Mr. Winslow would need two canes, Mrs. Winslow would need three purses, Kate would need a "Votes for Women" sign to carry into the drawing room in the third act, and so forth. She would help find the props, but after one was found, the actor who used it would be responsible for it.

They pulled their chairs in a circle and read through the first act. Erika hated how soft she was talking and kept waiting for the Stork to tell her to talk louder, but he didn't. When they were done he said, "We're all going to need to work very hard." Then he told them what had happened five years ago at Palmer Street School, where they were putting on *Arsenic and Old Lace*. A kid name Hughie had ruined it for everybody by forgetting all of his lines on opening night.

"So if you feel yourself getting lazy, remember little Hughie and make sure you don't follow in his footsteps, shall we?"

Erika and Sonia walked out of the building together. It was getting dark. Carrie's mom was waiting in her car, and when Erika opened the door she saw a cardboard box on the backseat and smelled baked chicken and rice, which she had eaten a hundred times at Carrie's house. Mrs. Ives smiled at her. "Dinner, so you can work on your lines. Carrie would have come in the car with me, but she's at her dad's. She has a science fair project in his basement. Growing plants in the dark?"

Mrs. Ives put the car in drive and started driving. "She talks to them. Half the little shoots she tells how nice they are, and the other half she tells how bad they are. She wants to see if the ones she says sweet things to grow faster. I'm sure you know all about it."

Carrie didn't have a project.

Erika said nothing.

When she got to her dad's there was a letter in the mailbox from Jean.

Dear Erika,

Thank you for calling me Tuesday night. You did the right thing. My grandmother used to talk about how in her village in Poland nobody could be cruel or kind without everybody knowing it. These days, many of us pay no attention to how children are treated, and how they suffer.

My husband didn't wake up.

You are not the only one who worried about Jade's father that day. Kit, our office manager, saw what you saw and mentioned it to me before she went home.

People sometimes talk about how strong and tough children are and how much they can take, but I think a lot of kids fake being OK just trying to keep from going crazy. What do you think?

Sincerely,

Jean

P.S.: I have a copy of the report I mentioned to you from Dr. Gruenberg. The next time we see each other, you may want to see it. She thought Erika Nevski was an interesting person.

Erika put the casserole in the oven, but she didn't turn on the heat because it was her dad's late night at work. Instead, she called him and told him it was there so he'd wait to eat until he got home. She read the letter again, and then she took her script and underlined her first twenty-five lines and began to try to memorize them. Her idea was that if she learned twenty-five a day, which didn't seem all that many, she'd be able to go onstage in two weeks without having to carry the book around. Then she decided the best thing to do would be to read it all the way through so she'd know the story. Then Carrie called.

"I got some ideas about lines you could say to make your character sound more interesting. I'll tell you what they are later. I'm calling from my dad's, looking after my crop."

At ten, Erika's dad walked in the door looking beat. He was hungry and so was she, and they ended up finishing most of the chicken casserole. When they were done, he asked her to tell him about what her lawyer had said. To distract him, she said, "Did I tell you about the blocks?"

"What blocks?"

"At the Children's Law Center? The waiting room is like

a playroom, with toys and trucks and stuff, but the blocks are so banged up and worn down you can't make a tower. It keeps falling down. I was playing with a little girl there Tuesday. It was frustrating."

"Yeah?"

"Yeah."

"It's not right. Somebody should do something."

Dear Diary,

Here's something for you to think about. If the Stork tells me to talk louder tomorrow, and I hit myself on top of my head, would that help my volume? It works with our TV. The Three Stooges do it all the time. Why not?

What's the use of knowing your lines if nobody can hear you? It's really scary.

Frank kisses me in Act I when we get engaged and in Act III just before we break up. That's twice, in case you're having a hard time counting this late at night. I know he'll know all his lines before I do, but even that's good because him knowing his lines will make me work harder to learn mine. The Stork says it's not a good idea for us to kiss in rehearsals. He says he doesn't want us to get bored with it. Bored kissing Frank?

I don't want to take the script home with me Saturday because Bernie might see it. He knows about my real life. Why should I let him know about my make-believe life? He'd end up telling me about his previous life on the streets of London.

If he told me he was Jack the Ripper back then I'd believe him.

Maybe Jack the Ripper's intern.

Karen thinks she can't live without him.

She should be smarter than that.

She <u>is</u> smarter than that.

Love,

Erika

9

Mrs. Fine came at the beginning of rehearsal on Wednesday, six days later, touched Erika on the shoulder, and led her to the costume room. On the way she apologized. "We've had a week of rehearsals and you and I haven't looked at anything yet. You should have been the first person I did. Mr. Stork wants to be sure you look exactly right."

They went backstage to the costume room. There were three dresses on chairs in the corner. "Those are for Mrs. Winslow," she said. "She's very careful about what she wears, but she doesn't care if it's in fashion or not. She wants to be a little out of date. The brown's for the first act, the purple's for the second and third, and the pink's for the fourth. I've also found a large gray hat with a narrow brim and a huge black-and-white feather, for the day she goes to see little Ronnie's trial. We want Kate's mother to be amusing, but we don't want the audience to laugh at her."

She went to a long rack of dresses against the far wall. "Your mom called me and said the two of you had bought patterns and material. Could you bring them in, maybe Monday, and let me look at them?"

Erika knew that Mrs. Fine knew her mom wasn't going to produce anything. "Mom and I haven't completely picked out any patterns," she said. "Maybe having backups would be good, just in case."

Mrs. Fine nodded. "That's just what I think. We don't want Mr. Stork still wondering what people are going to wear the week before opening night. It's especially important to get your look right." She pulled out a long black skirt with a narrow green ribbon around the waist. "Kate's got a job in the city. She has to dress to face the world."

Mrs. Fine held the skirt high and shook it out. It was long and very narrow. "Five years ago for the spring musical we did *Meet Me in St. Louis*, and the oldest sister wore this. The Judy Garland part in the movie, if you've seen it. She stole the show. Of course, she also had a marvelous voice. She was a good deal shorter than you, but it's got nine inches of hem we can let out if we don't find something better. I want you to get used to walking in something really narrow that hobbles your ankles. It'll take a bit of wiggling to get into it, but put it on."

She went to close the door and locked it. "Nobody can come in. See how it fits and feels."

Erika took off her shoes and jeans, pulled the skirt on, and buttoned the waist in the back.

"That narrow green band will set off your hair. Walk over here."

Erika took a step and fell down.

Mrs. Fine came over and helped her up. "Practice at home. Tie a short piece of clothesline to your ankles and walk around, always standing very straight. When you get used to it, you'll feel like a lady from a hundred years ago."

Erika got her balance and began walking toward the door again. Mrs. Fine stayed beside her. "I'm going too slow," Erika said.

Mrs. Fine look her head. "No. Kate's in a hurry to do what's right, but she never rushes."

Erika reached the door and slowly turned and walked back. It took forever.

"Stop," Mrs. Fine said. "You can take it off now. I'll put your name on it. You know the Salvation Army store on Grand Avenue? You live near there, I think. They might have some things you can use. They always do."

Erika put on her jeans again and went back to the band room.

"Just in time," the Stork said.

They went through the scene where John tells Kate that

her father has given permission for them to marry. The Stork kept coming up behind Erika, grabbing her elbows, and moving her around like a shopping cart. Frank seemed to have an intuition about where to stand and how to move, so she tried to follow what he was doing, which got the Stork off her back and made her feel a little bit like she might become Kate if she kept working at it. They went over the same page again and again, stopping before the kiss each time. At the end the Stork got between them and said to her, "Erika, we need more sound out of you. Just because you're engaged to John at this point doesn't mean you have to whisper everything to him."

"Maybe I should knock myself on the head," she said.

"What?"

"Nothing," she said. "I'm sorry."

He stepped back. "Whatever it takes," he said. "Whatever it takes."

When the rehearsal was over, Erika found Mrs. Ives waiting in her car.

"Do you mind taking me home instead of to Dad's?" Erika said. "Mom's seeing my lawyer tonight, and she wants me to show her the way."

"Wherever you want to go, I'm your taxicab," Mrs. Ives said, and started driving. "Who was that you came out of school with?"

"Sonia Merrero."

"She's in the play?"

"Yes."

"She's not very pretty, is she?"

"She was in a car accident."

"How sad. Are you friends?"

"Sort of. Now."

"I'm sure you missed Carrie today. She's still going over to the basement of her dad's house for her science project. I think it's a little bit creepy. All those plants trying to grow in the dark, and her talking to them?"

"It's science, I guess," Erika said.

"Your lawyer has to see your mom and dad both, is that right?" Mrs. Ives asked.

"I guess."

"Does she want to get them together again?"

Erika hadn't thought of that, and the idea made her afraid. "They're fine the way they are," she said.

Jean was at the law center working on a report for the Putnam family court. At seven-thirty she heard Mrs. Nevski's voice and went down the hall to the waiting room. Erika was with her.

"My little girl has told me so many wonderful things about you, Jean," Erika's mother said. "She's such a busy girl she only had time to pick out one picture for you. It's in her backpack. It's from her baby time, when we were acting like one big happy family."

Erika took out an envelope and handed it to Jean.

"Thanks," Jean said. "Erika, you haven't met Attorney Ingles yet. Come with your mom and me as far as his office."

She led them down the hall and stopped in front of Oz's door, introduced them, and left Erika with him. Then she led Mrs. Nevski the rest of the way into her office, put the envelope on her desk and sat down.

"Roomy," Erika's mother said, running her hand along the edge of the conference table. "I didn't expect a lawyer doing your kind of work to have this much space." She stepped over to the corner window and looked up at the sky. "Very nice."

"Old factories have big windows. It's from the days when it was cheaper to run your furnace than to keep your lights on. Would you care to sit down?"

Mrs. Nevski went around the far corner of the conference table, squeezed between the computer and the corner window, leaned over Jean's shoulder, and said, "Call me Becky." Then she sat down on the edge of the client's chair, looking ready to jump up again.

"Now that I've met you and seen the Children's Law Center as it really is," she said, "I can only say how lucky Erika is to have you. I think it's wonderful to have a lady in court to make sure the right people get their fair share."

Jean looked out the window. "Fair share of what?"

Mrs. Nevski picked the envelope off the desk, took out the picture, and looked at it. "The only one who looks any good in this is my baby. She'll always be that to me. That's the way it is with all moms I guess. You have children?"

"Three," Jean said. "I'm sure, when you talk about shares, you don't want me to think you see Erika as something you own."

Mrs. Nevski flicked the picture with her little finger. "No, no, no. There she is at Rocky Neck Beach. We used to go once a week in the summer. They were happier times. Not that we were ever really happy. I never would have gone to Arizona if it wasn't for Erika's sister, Karen. She's got asthma. It was much better for her out there. Night and day."

"Can I get you some coffee?" Jean asked. "We don't have cups, just mugs."

"A mug is fine, but I don't drink coffee anymore. Hot tea would be nice. Herbal if you have it. With just a touch of honey?"

Jean took the picture from her and went down the hall toward the little kitchen. While she was waiting for the water to boil, she looked at the photo. Four people on the beach. Sand, towels, a pail and shovel, a picnic cooler with a collection of bread and cheese and soda cans on top. Mrs. Nevski had a pair of sunglasses perched on the top of her head; Mr. Nevski, with a mustache so black and square it looked painted on, was squinting; Karen was sitting between them with her legs folded and a towel in her lap; and Erika, with a pail in her left hand, was looking down at a dead crab in the sand in front of her.

The water boiled, Jean made the tea, put in a spoonful of honey, dropped the bag in the trash. Back in her office, she sat down and gave the mug to Mrs. Nevski.

"My lawyer, Mr. Klecko, says you're going to drop in on me soon," Mrs. Nevski said.

"I hope to."

"We were thinking you and your family might want to take advantage of our invitation to join us for Thanksgiving dinner. Didn't Erika pass it on?"

"It's very kind, thank you, but we usually go to my parents' house."

"How sad."

"We like them, so we enjoy it. Tell me, what do you think Erika needs the most?"

Mrs. Nevski took another sip and set the mug carefully on the table. "You have a big influence over that. Don't get me wrong, I'm glad. It's a good thing. So I guess it's all up to you. You're more important than anyone right now."

Jean shook her head. "The world is full of lawyers, Mrs. Nevski. Erika has only two parents. It's important what you think she needs."

Mrs. Nevski sat back in her chair. "What does she need? One thing, not to live with that man. I'm sorry, but that's the long and the short of it. I could tell you things about how he is, but I won't. One thing, she has to eat take-out food all the time. He doesn't give her a chance to cook, and she's the world's most wonderful cook. Turn her loose in the kitchen, she loves it. Roast chicken is her specialty. Do you like to cook? I'll get her to bring you her favorite recipe. When she's back home, everything will be a million times better for everybody. This is excellent tea. Now, do I get to ask you a question?"

"Yes."

"Thinking about Erika's long-term personal interest, I've come to the conclusion that it would be best for me to legally change my name back to my family name. Goddard instead of Nevski. It's just a better name in every way. Do you know if I'm going to have to pay a large fee for that? Erika would want to do it if I did. Goddard. It's simple and it's musical. How complicated would that be?"

"I'm sorry to say I don't know. The question has never come up. I believe Mr. Klecko is your attorney? He's associated with a very reliable firm. I'm sure he would give you the best possible advice. Has Erika told you she wishes to change her name?"

Mrs. Nevski's cheeks got bright red. Maybe it was the hot tea. "I haven't brought it up to her because I'm not allowed to see her much and we have a lot of things to do and talk over, but she will want to, I know that. She's the most loyal girl in the world. Would it be the same price for two as for one, do you think? Her half sister would want to change, too, which would make three. And of course Karen has a different last name. You ought to be able to put it all on the same paper for the same price, don't you think?"

"I really have no idea," Jean said.

"But that's a good idea, talking to my attorney about it. What shall we talk about now? I really feel so much at home here. I can stay and talk as long as you like. Was this meeting what you expected? I mean, was it better or worse than the one you had with her father? Has he been here yet? He can fool people, you know."

"Would you be willing to sit down with him and me here and talk about Erika's future?" Jean asked. "It might be very helpful to her."

"Did he say he wanted it?"

"I haven't asked him yet."

Mrs. Nevski grinned at her as if they were two girlfriends who had just played a trick on somebody they hated. "Which means he hasn't been here. Anyway, if he says yes, then it's possible I'd be interested. Did you think that's what I'd tell you?"

"I try not to guess what people will say. They always surprise me."

"I was just asking because it might help Erika if I knew how you thought I had done today, one mother to another. What sort of appearance I made. Have I surprised you more than most people?"

"No."

"Oh."

In fact, Mrs. Nevski hadn't surprised her at all.

A fat old dog with curly tan hair came around the corner of Oz's desk, looked up at Erika, stretched, yawned, walked out into the hall, shook himself, came back, and went behind the desk again. Oz reached down to pet him.

"That's Max," he said. "I'm watching him for a client who's living in a motel room with his mom and two brothers at the moment. Max gets along with my dog at home as long as I'm there, but the neighbors say they bark at each other all day when I'm gone, so he comes with me." He took a picture of Rolph off his desk and showed it to her. "He's half poodle, half terrier, and half two other kinds of dog. I can't bring him into the office. He's a great dog, friendly, smart, but out of control. We're going to a dog obedience class one of these days so I can get trained on how to train him."

Erika heard Jean and her mom coming down the hall. Jean looked in. "Erika? Do you have a minute? If your mom won't mind waiting."

Jean led Erika down the hall to her office and closed the door behind them. "I have Dr. Gruenberg's report on you on my desk. You still don't remember visiting with her when you were in Mrs. Droste's class?"

Erika shook her head. "Sorry."

"Don't be sorry. It was a busy time for you. You can't control your memory."

Erika felt afraid. "What was wrong with me?"

"I can read you her description of how you were acting, if you'd like." Jean took it out of Erika's file folder. "Shall I? It's just a few sentences."

Erika looked toward the door to make sure it was shut. "Sure. Okay."

Jean read aloud from the top page.

During October, right after moving to her father's home, Erika demonstrated increasing anxiety, regression in her classwork, less interest in being with her peers, and general withdrawal from adults. Often, her facial expression became "flat," with little outward indication of what she was feeling at any time. This combination of withdrawal and lack of emotional expression was observed with concern by her classroom teacher, who attempted to engage her in conversations about what was troubling her, without success. Her classroom teacher described this shift in her behavior as a "collapse."

There were also episodes of extreme frustration and/or agitation. This seemed more directed internally than at other people. Occasionally she slammed books shut or appeared, through her facial expressions and body language, to be extremely agitated.

Erika felt herself blushing. She looked at her watch. "Mom's waiting."

Jean closed the folder. "Shall I make you a copy?"

"Not now."

"Okay. One more thing. Your mom was talking about you cooking when you're with her. She says you're very good."

Erika shrugged her shoulders. "I'm not all that good, really."

Jean looked at her intently. "They keep you pretty busy helping? Your parents?"

Erika shrugged again. "I don't mind. Well, I better go."

Sitting on the bus on the way home, her mom asked for a favor.

"It might sound silly to you, but I want you to go to the library and look in a cookbook for a good recipe for roast chicken, make a copy, and send it to Jean and say it's your favorite."

"Why?"

"I told her you love to cook roast chicken, and I'd get you to send her your favorite recipe."

"I should be there learning lines, Mom. I need to do twenty-five a day, and I'm not keeping up."

"You could do both things. How long can it take? One book. I'll give you the ten cents for the copy machine."

"It feels funny to fool my lawyer," Erika said. "It may even be illegal."

"Don't try to be Little Miss Honesty with me," her mom

said. "There are a million things you don't tell her. Isn't that right? I know you haven't told her Bernie stays over sometimes on the weekends and that he helps us out with money sometimes. Which is why we have a new antique jukebox, lights, bubbles, everything in perfect condition. Surprised? It's in the hall. You haven't seen it yet. Just got it yesterday. It's beautiful, with great old records. He's good to us. You should be grateful."

"He's a criminal, Mom. He's going to get arrested sometime, and maybe Karen, too, not that I'm saying she's doing anything wrong."

"I don't want to talk about him. Who needs to do that right now? I told this little lie about a chicken recipe, and I want you to make it true for me, that's all."

As the bus slowed, Erika started to stand up. Her mother grabbed her arm.

"Just answer me this," she said. "If I said one thing and Jean said another, which one of us would you believe? Never mind. Here's what you really need to know. She said she was going to make a home visit on us. A lightning attack, like they say on the History Channel. It could be this Sunday, so I want you to come early to help us clean up."

Erika nodded her head even though she knew Saturday morning Daddy would be making a birthday breakfast complete with cake.

"Be good. Here's a dime. Kiss me goodbye."

10

Erika's father took her to Goren's Sports at the mall Friday night to buy her a new pair of athletic shoes for her birthday. He liked the Nike ads, and that was the brand he wanted her to get. Luckily, the first pair looked great and fit exactly right. She kept them on and put her old shoes in the Nike box. They cost $89.99, which she knew her father couldn't afford, but there was no use trying to get him to buy her something cheaper.

They went to Angelo's for pizza. While they were waiting, she was afraid he was going to start knocking Carrie, which he loved to do, so she told him about Oz and his dogs.

"How many lawyers have you got? One's too many."

"Just got one. These shoes feel great."

"You call your lawyer a lot? Talk about a lot of things?"

"Not much. Now, with my new Nikes, if I need to talk to her, I can just run there and see her in person."

The waitress brought the pizza. Erika took a piece, but her dad just sat staring at it.

"Is that why you put them on right away, so you can get up and run and see her on a moment's notice? If that was the reason, it was a hell of a lot too much for me to pay."

Erika picked up the box, put the Nikes back in it, put her old shoes on, and went out to the car. It was locked, so she had to wait for him. When they got to the Dunkin' Donuts on Spencer Street, he drove around back, picked up the Nike box, got out of the car, and threw the box into the Dumpster.

Erika went to her room as soon as they got upstairs, shut the door, threw herself on the bed, and screamed into her pillow. When she was done she rolled over, took a deep breath, looked at the ceiling, and prayed to God to make at least one of her parents not insane. After a while she heard pans banging in the kitchen. Her father was making her birthday cake. Tomorrow morning when she went into the kitchen it would be in the middle of the table covered in plastic wrap that would stick to the frosting when she tried to take it off. She walked quietly to the bathroom and got ready for bed.

11

The next morning while she was packing to go home, Erika knocked her box of earrings down behind the dresser. She tried to move the heavy piece of furniture out from the wall, but over the years its feet had gotten stuck in the linoleum, so the easiest thing was to pull her suitcase out from under it and reach in. Her hand found most of the earrings, along with a lot of dust balls, but half of her best pair was missing. She went into the living room, where her father was watching TV, and asked him if she could borrow his flashlight. He got it for her and then stood at the door while she got down on the floor. She found the missing earring, plus one she didn't remember.

"Having that suitcase stuffed under there makes it look

like a motel room in here," he said. "It's like you're always on your way somewhere else."

She felt terrible. "I'm sorry, Daddy," she said. "I'm sorry about last night, too. I shouldn't have taken off your present. But you know, I'm not always running to see Jean."

"I don't know that. How could I? I don't know anything. Really. I know you sleep here six nights a week. Your mother left you to go off to Arizona five years ago, and still your head's somewhere else. I don't get it. Maybe I'm not supposed to. You want me to drive you to your mother's? Your lawyer thinks I should do stuff like that."

She shook her head and put her arms around him and kissed him and started to cry. "Thanks," she said when she got control of herself. "The bus is fine."

They went into the kitchen. There on the table, next to the cake, was the Nike box, banged in at one end and with a big streak of red jelly on it. She opened the box, took out the shoes, and put them on.

Her dad was smiling and crying.

"How'd you get them?" she asked.

"After the cake was finished I got that flashlight out and drove to the Dumpster and climbed in. Lucky it wasn't full. They must empty it Wednesdays or Thursdays. You wouldn't think old doughnuts would stink. It was easier getting in than getting out. The sides were slippery, but I made it. I took a shower when I got home so I wouldn't smell like a piece of cheese. I don't, do I?"

She shook her head and kissed him again. "No. You smell fine. I'll make you breakfast before I go home."

"No way," he said. "I get to make your birthday breakfast every year until you've got a husband to do it for you, and he better be willing to do it or I'll punch his lights out."

When Erika got home, her mom was standing at the bathroom door with a toilet brush in her hand. "Your lawyer thinks she's going to surprise us, but we're ready. It looks like a picture from *House Beautiful*, right? That's my birthday present to you, making the place look perfect. Bernie helped us roll the jukebox into the kitchen closet. I never saw him get out of bed so early in my life. He and Karen did the job and were gone by seven-thirty. Fits like the closet was made for it. I think there must have been a refrigerator in there once. The flat-screen TV we can say is one of those rent-to-buy deals, even if she tells us that's a terrible way to spend our money. It's not her business to give us good advice about how to spend our money, right? The trouble is, it makes it look like I've got money to burn. Let's see what's on TV."

They sat in the living room watching cartoons. Erika's mom pushed the mute button when the first commercials came on.

"What kind of legal advice does she give you?"

Erika shrugged her shoulders.

"Really. Tell me. Maybe I could use it sometime."

"She said to always write stuff down."

Her mom kept her eyes on the TV. "What stuff?"

"Ideas."

Her mother looked at her. "Like what?"

"Whatever I think of."

"They pay her to give you advice like that? I could tell you that. You need advice you can use now. Something that can really help you. Bernie says he's going to teach you ways to memorize things as his birthday present."

"I'm doing fine," Erika said.

Her mom shook her head. "I can tell when you're lying."

At eleven, Jean came. She stayed for an hour listening to Mrs. Nevski talk about Arizona and why she was glad to have come back home to her roots. When she was saying goodbye, Erika's mom brought up Thanksgiving again.

"Now remember, Jean, you and yours still have an invitation to Thanksgiving dinner. I know you said you always go home to your family, but they would all be welcome. No turkey. It will be Erika's famous chicken. Ten times better than the Colonel's. Which reminds me, Erika was going to send you her favorite recipe. She has two things on her list, send recipe and star in play."

Jean looked at Erika. "I got it in the mail yesterday."

"I knew that," Mrs. Nevski said.

Jean left, and Erika and her mom went into the kitchen.

"Well," her mom said, "that wasn't as bad as you thought it would be, was it? That woman must have had awful acne when she was your age. I'll bet the crybaby made you eat chocolate cake this morning, which is the worst thing a girl can eat. She didn't even look at the TV. Maybe she's got one herself."

Bernie and Karen soon came in and sat at the table. They had been across the street at Remy's Diner waiting, so they knew when Jean left. Bernie lit a cigarette and looked at Erika. "So, how's the memorizing work going?"

"Fine," she said.

"Your mom says it's more than three hundred lines." He covered his eyes with his hand. "Ask me to tell you what's on the countertop to the left of the sink. Never mind, I'll do it anyway. Two cans of corn, a fork, the sponge from the sink, and seven toothpicks. How do I know? Confidence. That's what remembering stuff's about. You just got to find a way to get that confidence, and I can help you there, too. There's a pharmacy product. It's new, but doctors are giving it out. Accudane. The chemical name is sedoxidex. It gives you that extra bit of energy and confidence."

Erika wanted some, and wanting it made her afraid.

"I'm fine," she said.

Bernie shook his head, smiling through his bad teeth.

"Like, if you know for sure you're going to remember somebody's name, you remember it. It's automatic. But if you think just maybe when the time comes you're going to forget it, you forget it. See what I mean?" He reached into his pocket and took out a small drugstore bottle. "Sedoxidex. It had extensive clinical trials before they let doctors prescribe it as Accudane. The results are amazing. Take two or three and all of a sudden you know you're going to get it done. You could take twice that without it hurting you." He held up his hands. "You're fine? Fine. But if you feel like you're just about to lose it, you want to deal with it right away, right? And don't look at me that way. It's not like it's a drug I picked up from some guy on the street. It's a chemical, from a doctor's prescription, a pharmacy. I'm going to put a little bottle in your backpack. Insurance."

12

After she got ready for bed, Erika unlocked her suitcase and took out the letter Karen had sent her before she and her mom came back from Arizona.

Dear Erika Grace,

Even if I have never written to you before, I still miss you. You are my sister!

I have not seen you for years. Now you are already a teenager! How time flies. I am here in Arizona (AZ) with our mother, and I hate to have to write it to you but things are not very good right now.

Our Mother (Mom from now on) wants to go back there, and so do I too. My x boyfriend that I have had here for a long long time turns out not to even <u>start</u> to care for me the *way a true boyfriend should do it. He makes the opposite sex back at Cooledge High when I was there look like they were all Prince Charming.*

But what I want to say is you as her child must miss our Mom and want to help her. It is your turn now, I'm sure you think when you think about it. I have been with her ever since we came out to AZ. I know you think the way I do. So think about it, and when we get back come and live with the two of us, because I have done my part and more, and then I could move out.

Sincerly, Your Sister,

Karen

P.S. Have you seen Bernie Markee? He was a senior at Cooledge the year I decided to stop going evry day. I think he liked me, and then the troubel was we went away. Can you look up his number in the telephone book for me and see if he's still around? He'd wink at me like he liked me. Thanx.

Erika sat on her bed holding the letter in her lap. At the time, she had looked Bernie up in the phone book without finding him. She tore the letter into tiny pieces and flushed it down the toilet.

13

Dear Diary,

Before rehearsal began today, the Stork told us the band needed the room so we had to start using the auditorium right away. It wasn't supposed to be for two more Mondays. Then when we got there, he turned on the sound system. I hate mikes. You know what I mean by the word hate? I hate them. He said we shouldn't pay any attention, just to talk the way we always talk. How could we, with our voices bouncing all over the walls??? All my lines sounded like they were coming from somebody else. The ones I remember, I mean. It's scary.

Love,

Erika

14

When Jean got to the office Tuesday, there was a message from Jack Klecko. She dialed his number hoping he wouldn't be there, but he was.

"Jean, thanks for calling me back. How are things going?"

"Fine. How about you?"

"Terrific. The best. Here's my idea. You and I are already on the same page as far as Erika and my mom go. We could go into court tomorrow and we'd find out we agree on everything. You get the father on board, we write out an agreement, we go in front of Judge Gifford, and ten minutes later we're done and everybody's happy, seewumsane?"

Jean pulled out Erika's file and turned over the few pages in it, the assignment sheet, her notes on her talks with Erika and her home visit, a page headed "Mediation Meeting" with nothing but the date on it, school records, the report from Dr. Gruenberg. She closed it. "Have you been in touch with Mr. Nevski?" she asked.

"Me? With Erika's father? That's more your job than mine. I mean, your client's living with him. He's got to know she wants to live with my mom. Of course, with a visitation schedule he can live with. A dad's got rights, right? You think he's going to give us a hard time? I wish he had a lawyer, so the three of us could get together. I think you'd be the one to get him in line. His ex hates him, but he's not a bad guy, as far as I can tell. I mean, you can understand where he's coming from, seewumsane? So maybe you could talk with him, just the two of you. You had them together already before, right?"

"Not yet."

"Who needs it? I just call my mom and tell her you're going to sit down and talk with him sometime in the near future and work out a plan, you know, a schedule that's fair to everybody. She's ready to be reasonable as long as he's not in the same room. What do you say?"

Jean shook her head. "Erika's got a big part in a play, which is taking all her attention, and I'm still not ready to say what she wants."

There was silence for about five seconds. "Really? It's so simple. My mom and Erika have both wanted to be together for years and years. You think she's going to change her mind? There's something I should tell you. My mom, for some reason, don't ask me why, has gotten the idea into her head that you've been telling Erika what she should think. I told her that we've known each other for years, and you would never do such a thing."

"Good."

"We have to stick together, seewumsane? So, how soon do you think we can finalize the new custody plan?"

Jean closed Erika's folder and looked out the window. "Not next week, Jack."

"That's not the way I see it at all. My client says your client knows exactly what she wants, and I think my client's right."

Dear Diary,

In English today Heinz was going over things people used to say that are completely changed now. Now we say "I could care less," but we used to say "I couldn't care less," which is the opposite. Also people talk about "pulling yourself up by your own bootstraps," which is impossible, but now it means "work hard and you'll succeed." The only thing you can get from pulling on your own bootstraps, he said, is a hernia. Still, it's a nice idea that you can do anything you want if you just reach down and pull hard. Stupid, but nice.

Good night,

Erika

15

Wednesday morning Jean went to court on two cases in which she was the children's guardian. The cases were very similar, and in each one she had gotten the parents to reach an agreement and put it in writing. After the first case, the mother and father walked out of the courtroom by different doors, both of them hating her for what they thought she'd made them do, so she knew they'd be back fighting before the end of the year. After the second case, the parents came over to her and told her she was the best friend their child had ever had. Case closed? Maybe. She could hope.

After the second hearing she took the elevator up to the fourth floor and walked into the office of Karli Hest, who did all the court scheduling. Everybody loved Karli. She was smart, she knew her job, and she didn't play favorites among the attorneys, even though she knew which ones to trust and which ones to doubt. On the wall behind her desk was a bulletin board full of pictures of dogs—judges' dogs, lawyers' dogs, friends' dogs, her own dogs, and a few strays. They all had their names written underneath. Oz's shaggy dog was there, with *Rolph Ingles* under it.

Karli looked up from her computer and smiled. "Your friend Mr. Jack Klecko called me up this morning about the Nevski case. He said you were close to an agreement, and you might be ready in two weeks."

Jean smiled. "Mr. Klecko dreams dreams."

"You won't be?"

"No. The dad's in no hurry. He's coming to my office Saturday. I'm seeing her school guidance counselor today at three. She's starring in her school play with I don't know how many lines to learn. She needs to be on the calendar, but not too soon."

"When's the play?"

"The week before Thanksgiving."

"How about the week after that, the second of December at ten?"

"Fine."

At three, Jean was signing the visitors' book in the office at Hoover Junior High. Mr. Janik was in the coffee room waiting for her. He grabbed her hand and shook it.

"Janik. Guidance," he said. "I don't get to see lawyers every day of the week. There was a time when I never got to see them at all, but those were the good old days. What can I do for you? Coffee? Tea? Fruit juice? Pepsi?"

"No, thank you, I'm fine."

He reached into the refrigerator and took out a bottle of water, led the way to his office, and plunked the bottle down next to the guest chair. "No lady ever sits in my office without a refreshment in her hand. You're here about Erika Nevski. We're old friends. Lovely child. Smart, you know? But nervous. Where'd the secretary put her file folder?"

"Is it there?" Jean asked, pointing to a pile next to the phone.

"Right. The thin ones are always the hardest to find." He opened it and sat reading. After a minute Jean put her hand on the desk.

"May I?" she said.

He gazed at her sidewise, like a dog when you get too near his bone. It crossed her mind, for a second, that he might grab her hand and bite it. Then he closed the folder. "What is it you want to know?"

She put on what she hoped was a sweet smile. "Everything."

"There's not much. She's done very, very, very well here. Only the bad kids get thick files. I could show you some you could hardly carry, they're so heavy."

Jean kept smiling. He opened the file again but kept his pudgy hand on the corner of it. His fingernails were dirty. "See? All A's and B's and no detentions."

She took the file and looked through Erika's report cards.

"I always keep on top of my children," he said. "You probably don't know it, but she's got a big part in the fall drama production. Three weeks from tomorrow."

Jean looked back at him. "Really? How nice."

He reached out and took the folder back. "I like lawyers," he said. "They uphold the law."

Jean thanked him on behalf of all lawyers everywhere, said goodbye, and left his office. As she was signing out, a good-looking woman in very high heels came up behind her.

"I'm Ms. Marx. I'm also in guidance. Did you get everything you needed?"

"Thank you, I think so. I saw Erika Nevski's file. I assume there's only one?"

Ms. Marx smiled. "Yes. I ask you the question only because Mr. Janik is retiring in a few months, to New Mexico, where he has family, and his heart is already halfway there. Possibly his head, too. I'm glad he was of service to you. Erika's in the fall play. She's probably rehearsing now. It's better not to go in, but there are windows in the auditorium, where they're working. Shall I show you?"

"No, thank you," Jean said. "If Erika's rehearsing, I might just distract her."

When Jean got back to the office, there was a message on her answering machine from Mr. Nevski.

Hello. This is Erika's father. I just wanted to call to say I'm not one of these guys you women always talk about who always think they know what's right. But I know what's right for Erika and who takes care of her best and it's me. Well, have a nice day.

16

Erika stopped at McDonald's after rehearsal, so it was dark when she got to her dad's. Bernie was waiting for her out front, standing next to his car with a cigarette in his mouth. She saw him when she turned the corner. She wanted to duck back and go to the library, but he had seen her and taken two steps toward her, so she kept walking.

"Karen had a little asthma attack," he said when she got to him. "We thought we were going to have to take her to the emergency room." He threw his cigarette into the street. "She needs to give up smoking. She'd do it if you told her. Tell her."

"Is she all right?"

"Sure. Want to see for yourself? I'll take you home and

get you back here before your dad comes home from work, so he won't know."

She didn't want to get in his car, but she couldn't stand next to it and tell him she wanted to take the bus.

"I won't bite unless you ask," he said.

On the way home, Bernie stopped off for a quart of chocolate chip ice cream. "Karen asked," he said, dropping the bag in Erika's lap. "Sugar fiend."

He parked the car across from the apartment and followed her up the stairs. "Not such a awful ride, right, sis? No accidents in the streets."

While he was talking, Erika felt his spit spraying the backs of her ankles.

Karen was sitting at the kitchen table waiting for her ice cream. She looked fine. After kissing her and her mom, Erika sat down with a paper napkin and reached under the table to wipe her legs. She didn't know or care if Bernie was watching.

"What happened was I just ran out of breath," Karen said. "No problem. Bernie gave me this inhaler. One for my pocket and one for next to my bed. Combivent, the newest thing. The same as albuterol, only better. You get attacked by somebody in the street, you pull it out and point it at them and squirt it in their eyes, they go blind for a while. Nothing bad about it as long as you point it at your mouth. It's a regular prescription item. Nothing illegal. I don't remember the name of the ingredient that blinds people."

Bernie brought four bowls of ice cream and sat down. "Ipratropium."

Mrs. Nevski put the ice cream container in the freezer, came to the table, and smiled at Erika. "What do you think? Karen's pretty lucky, right?"

Bernie laid his arm across Karen's shoulder as if he owned her.

Erika looked at the clock over the stove. It was already twenty after eight.

"Don't worry," Bernie said. "I'll get you back to your dad's in plenty of time. Right now, what do you think of your sister? The same thing as everybody else. Lucky, right?"

Bernie got Erika home a minute before nine. "Your dad won't be here for another half hour, right? So what'll you do when you get upstairs?" He lit a cigarette, which gave her a reason to roll down her window. "Maybe you got a test coming up in something?"

Erika didn't answer.

"Studying your lines?"

"Sometimes."

"When it comes right down to it, you don't have any friends, do you, except me and Carrie, and I got one thing going for me she don't, which is I'm not crazy."

Erika opened the car door. "Carrie isn't crazy."

Bernie held up his hands. "You think I want to argue about her? No way. If you say so, Carrie's as sane as anybody else. She's as sane as I am. You want some advice? Think about who your real friends are. People who worry about you and help you out when you need it. People who help your relations. Think about them."

Erika said goodbye and ran upstairs.

17

Dear Diary,

It's Friday night. It's a long time since I wrote you. Sorry.

I went to the movies at the mall Sunday with a bunch of kids from the show. Frank was wearing a watch he got out of a cereal box, and we talked about the first time we got different stuff. I told him why I thought watches from cereal boxes would last longer than watches from the dollar store, even though the bands aren't as good. (HINT: The batteries are newer.) I did more talking than he did, and I laughed a lot. Is that a good thing? I don't want him to think I'm crazy.

Maybe because I wanted him to know I could be serious I told him about lying in bed when I was a kid and wondering if the world was real. He said the same thing happened to him. He might have just been trying to be nice. I wanted to say to him, are you real, but I didn't.

Smart, right?

We still don't kiss in the rehearsals.

Rehearsals are in the auditorium now, and the stage crew's almost done with the set.

The Stork doesn't like me.

I think I'll ask Sonia to find out if Frank likes me. His hair's growing long, so he's going to have to cut it again to look like John. Mrs. Fine's got a real British Army uniform for him. She first thought a band uniform from another school would work, but band uniforms, surprise surprise, look like band uniforms.

I'm going to bed now. Daddy's seeing Jean tomorrow.

Love,

Erika

P.S. Carrie cut social studies and came into fourth-period lunch and said we should go to the mall next Sunday with nobody else.

18

Erika's dad had five pairs of chino pants and five work shirts. Every day when he came home from work he took off the shirt and pants he was wearing, put them in the hamper, took a shower, and put on the next day's shirt and pants. If he wasn't too tired, he shaved at the same time so he'd be ready to go in the morning, but sometimes he put it off until after dinner and watching TV.

Weekends he wore jeans.

He also had the suit he got married in, plus two white shirts and a hanger full of ties that had belonged to his father. On Saturday morning when Erika came out of her room with her backpack, ready to go home, she found him in the kitchen all dressed up. Then she remembered he had a date to see Jean. She told him he looked nice but he might want to trim his mustache a little bit.

"You think it's getting shaggy?"

"I don't like it square the way it used to be," she said, "but it's getting to look a little raggedy."

Jean walked into her office with a jelly doughnut and a large coffee at five after nine. Mr. Nevski was due at ten, but she guessed he was the kind of man who always tried to get places early, and she wanted to be there when he arrived. She sat at her desk and worked on a *guardian ad litem* report she had to file by the following Wednesday, looking out the window at the parking lot every once in a while. Then a red convertible drove in and a tall man got out. Jean went to meet him. When she got to his car, he was taking a big cardboard box out of the trunk.

He looked at her and smiled. He was thin, his hair was turning gray, there was a little red in his mustache, and he looked unhappy. "These are for you," he said. "Erika said your building blocks are terrible. Worn down so they don't stack, right?"

"Erika'd know," she said. "She was down on the waiting room floor with a three-year-old named Jade a few weeks ago."

Mr. Nevski shook the box. "The former landlord made them in the cellar for his kid, and then his wife ran away with the kid so he took off and left them behind. Some parents, you just don't know what they're thinking about. The new owner doesn't do anything but come around once a month and collect the rent. Not that the building's unsafe or anything, and even if it was I have two smoke alarms in my apartment. They're all hardwood. The blocks. So they won't splinter or anything."

"Our clients thank you. That's a beautiful car."

"It's my pride and joy. After Erika, I mean. She comes first with me in everything. It's a 1962 Thunderbird. What they called the Sports Roadster. Three-hundred-and-ninety-horsepower V-8 engine. Original white leather seats."

"It looks brand-new."

"I do my best to keep it up. Let a vintage car start to slide and it costs you thousands to bring it back. I've had offers. My boss wants to buy it. There weren't too many sold. You don't see them much on the road."

She led the way to the building. "The blocks look heavy."

"You should get rid of the old ones. I'll haul them away for you."

"Thanks."

"No problem."

He followed her up the stairs into the old building. In the waiting room he put the box down in the corner next to the toy chest, and they went into Jean's office.

"Did you happen to bring the parent information form with you?"

He slapped his pockets. "I got it somewhere. I don't know where. I don't wear this jacket all that much."

She took out a blank form, put it in front of him, and laid a ballpoint pen on it. "Maybe you could fill it in now while I go make us some coffee?"

She took her time. When she went back, the form was filled out. Without looking at it, she put it in Erika's folder.

They talked about the weather and the Red Sox. He sat at attention like a little boy called to the principal's office for doing something bad in class.

"I haven't used that word in front of Erika since that night we talked," he said all of a sudden. "Not because I was afraid she'd tell on me, either. She doesn't do stuff like that."

"A loyal daughter."

"You could put it that way."

"How do you think she's doing?"

"What do you mean?"

"How do you think her life is going?"

"The two of us get on great. We always got on great. She has a big part in the school play. The bitch—" He stopped and looked down and then around at the office walls. "I didn't mean that. It's the first time I said it since you warned me. Her mother claims she's going to make all her costumes, but she'll never do it."

"Maybe you can think of some things to do to relieve some of the stress on Erika?"

"I don't give her any stress. If you're worried about stress, keep her out of the way of her mother. Maybe you can get the judge to do that."

"What does she need most of all? What would make her life better?"

"I just told you. Other big stuff?"

"Big. Small. In between. Whatever. Just, what do you think she needs?"

"A new TV. But that's taken care of. We're getting one delivered today. This afternoon. It's a surprise. When Erika comes back to me tomorrow, it'll be sitting in the living room with the cable connected. It's a Panasonic with a built-in DVD player. I should go to the flower department at Stop & Shop and get one of those silk bows you can stick on presents."

"Since that's taken care of, what else?"

"Personal?"

"Personal."

"She could use a different best friend than the one she's got. Carrie Ives got her hooks in her four years ago and won't let go. Crazy family. Father and mother both have big houses in the hill section. All money and no brains. I hear Erika on the phone. I mean I don't hear her much because Carrie talks and she listens. Her father's some executive in one of the big insurance companies. We do body work on police department cruisers. Bullet holes. Really. If the cruiser's new enough so they want to keep it. I got a friend there. He says Carrie's on her way to being a criminal."

"They made friends in fifth grade," Jean said.

Mr. Nevski leaned back. "How'd you know?"

Jean shrugged. "Erika's my client, Mr. Nevski. I'm supposed to know things like that."

The phone rang at Kit's desk in the waiting room. The answering machine was on, so Jean didn't need to get up and answer it, but she was glad for the excuse to let him think a little more. It was a Law Line call, a woman who said she needed advice about getting a restraining order against her husband. The conversation took a while. When Jean went back in the office, Mr. Nevski was looking down into his empty coffee mug.

She put her hand out. "I have more made if you'd like," she said.

"No, thanks. I want you to get it straight about the Iveses. It's not that I've got anything personal against them. Mrs. Ives is the closest thing Erika has to a real, decent mom. She cooks for her, for God's sake. She gives Erika rides places. Half the time she brings her home from rehearsal, but still it would be better if the whole family got lost. You want to know the truth, I feel sorry for them. I mean, him and her aren't to blame for having somebody like Carrie for a child."

"Anything else you can think of Erika needing?"

"Money. That's another reason Carrie's no good for her. Erika goes to Carrie's house and she can see the difference between what I can give her and what they have to throw around. That's about it."

He shrugged his shoulders and sat silent, and Jean knew there was something else he wanted to say. She waited. He brushed down his mustache with his fingers. "There's something Erika could decide to do for me if she wanted, and it would be good for the both of us, me and her, too. Every time I try to tell her about what happened between her mother and me, just so she'll know how it was and who's to blame, she gets up and walks away. When she was little I could hold on to her, but even then whenever I tried to tell her stuff she'd scream and put her fingers in her ears. If you told her to listen to my side, she might do it. I know she listens to the mother's side, so why shouldn't she know the truth?"

"I don't think you're right about that," Jean said. "I don't think she wants to hear either side. Why should she?"

"It's like the Bible says, the truth shall make you free, and I could show up her mother's lies. I mean, it's Erika's life, what went on with me and her mother before the divorce."

"No, it's not her life, Mr. Nevski, it's your life, and your ex-wife's. Most of what's said in divorce and custody proceedings is either boring or nasty. Don't tell her horror stories. I don't care if they're true or not. Do something nice for her instead. Drive her to her mom's in your beautiful red Thunderbird some Saturday morning."

He looked out the window. "I already offered and she said no, which is a good thing because I haven't got a lot of time to drive anybody anyplace, and besides, it's mostly weather like this. Plus she likes the bus. And if she's going to see her mom and it's raining or snowing or something, she can stand in the downstairs hall and see it coming. She's happy the way things are. She doesn't want to give me more trouble than I already have." He looked at her hard. "Do I get a turn to ask you something?"

"Sure."

"Has my ex been here like I am now? She always has to get her licks in first. What she told the judge at our divorce? It was all the same old lies. You know, if you don't want me to tell Erika the truth about the divorce, I could tell you and you could tell her."

Jean took a deep breath and let it out slowly. "With all due respect, Mr. Nevski, if I thought I needed to know the testimony at your divorce hearing four years ago, I would order a copy of the court transcript. In fact I already have."

"When you read it you'll know what a bitch she is," he said. "That's all I want." He started to stand up. Jean stayed in her chair looking at him, and he sat back down again.

"Would you be willing to meet her here, the three of us, to have a discussion about Erika's future?"

"Did you ask her?"

"Yes."

"What did she say?"

"She might be interested."

"What does she mean, 'interested'?"

"It's just the word she used, Mr. Nevski. I can't say exactly what she meant. I think she wondered if you'd be willing."

"Sure. I'm not afraid. I'll do it. But right in here, with you in the room all the time. And I don't want to run into her in the parking lot. I want to get here before she comes and be out of here before she goes."

"I can arrange the first half. When people choose to get up and go I have no control over."

"Okay." He stood up. "Just let me know."

Jean smiled. "More coffee? There's plenty."

"No. Thanks."

"I had a visit with Erika's fifth-grade teacher, Mrs. Droste," Jean said. "She had a copy of Erika's class picture. Your daughter had short hair at the time."

"When she started living with me, I didn't want to have to make braids every day and she didn't know how to do it right back then, so I took her to the beauty parlor."

"Mrs. Droste said she cut it in the girls' room at school."

"Well, that's where she started working on it, only because the class was so boring she had to do something to keep herself busy, and then I trimmed it some more, and then we went to the beauty parlor and got the job finished. I like it short."

"It looks nice both ways," Jean said. "Okay, we're done. Thanks for coming in."

He took away the old blocks and Jean sorted the Saturday

mail. People sent the law center donations, sometimes with letters and sometimes not, so she had a Christmas-in-July feeling every time she opened the envelopes. There was no money, but the transcript of the Nevski divorce hearing was there. She went back in her office, opened it up, and read through it quickly.

When Erika unlocked the door and went in, Karen and her mom were having their every-other-Saturday-morning fight in Mom's bedroom. There was a smell of garbage and paint in the air. Erika stood in the hall listening to find out what the argument was about. It was simple. Bernie had gotten them a roast chicken on Wednesday, and one of them had put the bones in the garbage instead of taking them down to the big can in the basement, and now the kitchen stank. To judge from the volume, the fight had just begun. Erika had learned that trying to stop them too early only made them switch to a fight about something that had happened in Arizona, and those fights always ended up with them giving each other the silent treatment for days.

She went into her room and shut the door. The walls were painted Sunny Umbrella. It was a little streaky, so you could see the old green paint underneath in some places, but it was nice.

Mom is sure she'll get me, she thought.

She took off her backpack, opened the window, and stood looking down at the dirt yard while the cold morning air blew in. After a minute she got her script out and sat on her bed and tried not to listen to the fight, but it didn't work. She waited. When she heard her mom and Karen go into the kitchen, she walked between them, grabbed the plastic garbage bag, took it downstairs, and dumped it. When she got back, they had opened the windows to get out the smell and were starting to make Jell-O instant pudding, giggling and bumping hips as they passed each other.

"So, how do you like it with a sunny yellow room?" her mom asked.

"It looks great," Erika said, and went over and kissed her.

"Karen still has to do the door."

"It's fine the way it is. I like it green."

"But you're glad the walls are yellow."

"They're great."

A key turned in the lock. It was Bernie, with his daughter, Claudia, in his arms. He put her on the hall floor, came into the kitchen, kissed Karen, and tugged at her mother's bathrobe belt.

"Becky, what's going on? I called ten times on my cell phone. You always turn the ringer off, so how can you expect to get calls? Nobody ever answers the goddam phone around here even when it's on. Why have one if you just let it ring all the time?"

He grinned at Erika. She walked past him into the living room and opened the closet door, looking in just to have something to do. As she stood there, Bernie came up behind her and slid his fingers lightly over the back of her neck so she jumped forward into the winter coats. When she recovered her balance and turned around, he clapped his hands and grinned at her.

"We're making progress," he said. "At least this time you didn't try to cut my throat with your bracelet."

Karen was watching from the doorway. She grabbed Erika's hand, pulled her down the hall into the kitchen, and pushed her against the sink. "We need to get some things straight," she said. "Right now. Not later. Right now. Do you remember those leather shoelaces? I know you do. The ones you took out of my loafers where they ran around the edge so you could make some stupid bridge project for school? Which you never asked me for and said you were going to pay me for but didn't?"

"I thought I paid," Erika said.

"Well, even if you did, which you didn't, you ought to know you can't make something like that good just with money."

"I'm sorry."

Karen leaned closer to her, pushing her back against the edge of the sink. "Bernie's not a pair of shoelaces, you know. You're not going to take him away from me."

"I don't want him."

"You think you're too good for him? You do, don't you? Admit it."

It was true, Erika did think she was too good for him, and

too young, and too smart, but she couldn't say any of that. She looked down at Karen's feet.

"What are you looking at?"

"I'm sorry," Erika said.

"You always say you're sorry and it never does anybody but you any good. What are you sorry for?"

"I don't know. Making you unhappy, I guess."

"What would give you an idea like that? You can't make me unhappy. You could before, but not anymore. But you can do something for me. Right now. Today. Will you?"

"Sure, if I can."

"You're going to tell the judge you want to come home, right?"

"I have to get my lawyer to do it."

"It's the same thing, right? You tell the lawyer, the lawyer tells the judge, and it happens. I want you to tell Bernie, *now*, that when you come home you'll be taking my place and I can go whenever he's ready. I watched out for Mom for all my life. It's time for me and him to get a place of our own and have a life."

"I don't think what I say will make any difference to him."

"Yes it will. He listens to you. And Mom's going to be glad to get rid of me. She thinks you're her salvation. It's your turn, Erika."

Karen turned to go back in the living room, but Erika reached out. "Where'll you go? Will you move in with Bernie?"

"Not right away. He has to live with his ex-wife most of the time for now. She says she's going to have another baby, and if it turns out to be true, he doesn't think it's right for him to leave her alone right now. It's not his baby, I know that."

"How do you know?"

"He told me. He swore it was the truth. The important thing is you being here, ready for when the time comes. He likes the idea, too, so that's all of us."

Erika turned to the sink and started washing the dishes. She didn't want Karen to see how shocked and mad she was. Shocked by Bernie's lies, even though she knew what kind of man he was, shocked that Karen would believe him, and mad that Karen let him own her, body and soul. She felt as if the kitchen had turned into the street and a truck was heading straight for her.

Bernie hung around the living room until Claudia got cranky, and then he got up. Karen followed him to the door and looked at Erika.

"Bernie?" Erika said. "When I get back home, Karen's going to be free to fly."

"What's that mean?"

"So that you two can get your own place."

"Yeah? Well, as soon as we can. Apartments cost plenty. Besides, you'd miss me if she moved out."

After they left, Erika picked up Claudia, carried her into her room, put her down on the bed with the blanket across her, rubbed her back, and sang the *Sesame Street* theme to her over and over. When she was asleep, Erika looked down at her. After a while she thought of another good reason for coming home. She could leave the ringer on and answer the phone when somebody was calling.

When Jean got home from the office, she found a large envelope in her mailbox. There was no return address on it. She opened it up. Inside was a child's diary. The cover was pink, with a picture of Alice in Wonderland sitting next to a cactus. Clipped to it was a note on pink paper.

Dear Ms. Rostow-Kaplan,

My daughter told me you gave her a diary as a present. Hooray for you! I hope she will use yours for words instead of just pictures, but she was just a little girl back then and the pictures she made are wonderful. I keep listening for your next phone call to arrange our next meeting! We have so much to talk about! I hope to see you again very soon!

Sincerely yours,

Becky

It took her a few seconds to remember that Mrs. Nevski's first name was Rebecca. She looked up her number and dialed it. Erika answered. "Hello?"

"Erika, I didn't expect you. Of course, it's Saturday so you're there. I'm calling to speak with your mom."

"I'll get her."

There was a long wait, and then Mrs. Nevski picked up the phone.

"Jean, how nice to hear from you! What can I do for you?"

"Two things. Would you be free to meet with me and Mr. Nevski tomorrow afternoon? At four? I think it might be in Erika's interest."

"Is that what he said he wants?"

"He might be available then, if you could be."

"I'd love it."

"I'll call Mr. Nevski right now, then," Jean said. "If he can't make it, I'll let you know. Otherwise we'll get together at the office at four."

"Fine."

"I'll see you then. The other matter is that I received Erika's diary. I'm sure the pictures are wonderful, as you say, but I don't feel I should open it without her permission. Shall I give it back to you tomorrow when we meet?"

"Good idea," Mrs. Nevski said. There was an edge in her voice. "It's one of my treasures."

19

Jean stood in her office looking at her conference table, which she had just cleared of files and law journals and a large, heavy paper cutter that Kit had put there for some reason. Out her window the sky was gray. A cold wind was blowing, and maybe a few snowflakes, she wasn't sure. Still, across the street in the playground kids were playing basketball in their T-shirts.

The table was long, dark, and heavy. It would have been better round, like the one in her kitchen at home. Anyway, it was work furniture, and Erika's parents were coming there to get work done.

She looked at her watch and then out at the parking lot. At ten minutes to four Mr. Nevski drove through the gate in his red Thunderbird and parked almost directly under her office window. She went to the table and moved one of the chairs back a few inches. She left the office and went through the waiting room to meet him, and when he rang the bell she brought him into her office and went back out so Mrs. Nevski wouldn't find them together.

Mrs. Nevski came.

Jean began. "This meeting isn't about either one of you, what you've done or said or felt in the past. It's about finding ways to help Erika, your daughter, be happy and successful. So talking about what either of you said or did in the past is out of bounds."

Mr. Nevski stood up. "It's all about what she did," he said. "If you don't want to hear about it, I'm out of here."

Jean sat silent, waiting.

He left.

Mrs. Nevski smiled into her tea mug. "So," she said, "you see what kind of man he is. At least he didn't start crying. That's something anyway."

Two minutes later, she was out the door, too.

As soon as Mrs. Nevski was gone, Jean called Karen and asked if they could meet for lunch at the McDonald's on Bethlehem Avenue.

Jean got there first and sat in a booth near the counter, looking out the window. When Karen came, she got a tray full of food at the counter, but after she sat down she just picked at her fries. "Erika's probably told you a lot about me," she said.

Jean shook her head and smiled. "Not much," she said. "I know she likes you."

Karen pushed her tray aside. "I'm going back to school for computers," she said. "I was taking a real high-level course, intense, last winter, but then I got sick, and when I got better they wouldn't let me back in."

"How long were you sick?"

"A long time. Also, I have to take care of Mom all by myself. I don't get much help from Erika. She thinks her life is the only thing in the world to think about. I guess you know we were out west for a while. It was Mom, really, and not getting any help from Erika, that kept me from finishing the course."

"What do you think would be best for Erika?"

Karen's face puffed up with anger. "Why should that be the big thing? Next to the rest of us, what's she got to worry about? Send her home is all. Girls belong with their moms. There are a lot more years between me and Erika than it might look like. I'm twenty-four already. Most of the girls I went to school with are out on their own now. I would be, too, maybe. If."

Jean waited for a few seconds. "If what?" she asked.

"If a lot of stuff. He may not be my real daddy, but someday I'm going to go over there and tell him how he's ruined my life. In high school I was a very promising person with a lot of potential," she said. "My guidance counselor came right out and told me that. Right now, today, I could go places."

"What's getting in your way?" Jean asked.

"It's true, most of my good friends are older. Not a lot older, but I need my own apartment. Erika should be with Mom full-time. She's got her own room out of the way, bathroom, kitchen right there. She could have her happy little life like now and be with Mom at the same time and help her out once in a while."

"Does your mom need help?" Jean asked. "I was with her a little while ago, and she seems very well. Is there a difficulty I don't know about?"

"No, nothing." Karen smiled, put her mouth on the straw of her Coke, and slurped. "There's plenty of food here," she said. "You want some?"

"No, thanks," Jean said.

"Mom could eat everything on this tray and beg for more," Karen said. "Talking about Erika? She looks like the nicest little girl, which I'm not saying she isn't, but it's another big point why she should come home. That's what she needs. Ask her, she'll tell you." Karen waved her hand in the air the way her mom did, and then sat back. "I have to go meet somebody now. Anything you want of this, feel free."

She got up and left.

Jean sat still a few minutes feeling sad and discouraged. How can you keep a client from running into a burning building if that's what she thinks she has to do?

She slid out of the booth, dumped the tray, drove home, and went to watch Martin and Nathan play soccer.

20

At four, Carrie picked up Erika to go to the mall. She was driving her father's new white Saab convertible. Around four-thirty they went to the hardware section of Target, and two minutes later a security guard was standing between them with his hand on Carrie's shoulder. Carrie turned to Erika and smiled. "He thinks I'm trying to steal something," she said with her eyes wide. The security guard, an old guy with a flat nose, looked at Erika and said, "You better come to the manager's office too, girlie."

On the way, Erika felt Carrie's hand pushing her father's car keys down into her pocket. She turned toward her, but Carrie was looking the other way and telling the man that she had already paid for the pliers, which were for her father's birthday, and thrown away the cash register tape in one of the mall trash bins, she couldn't at the moment remember which one, and she had come back to the store because she suddenly remembered that he wanted her to get him a screwdriver, too. "Of course I don't mean the word *get* in the larceny sense," she said. "I meant *buy*."

The security guard held up the cut package, waved it in front of her face, and told her it would go easier with her if she gave him the razor she'd done the cutting with so she wouldn't have to be searched. Carrie smiled and gave him the cutter, blade first. "This is mine," she said. "So I expect it back." Then she turned her head, looked down at Erika's pocket where she'd put the keys, and said in a loud voice, "Daddy's going to be really mad when he gets back home unless everything is exactly the way he left it." Erika bit her lip and shook her head. Carrie leaned toward her and whispered, "It's automatic. Just start it and go."

They were near the manager's office. People were staring at them. Erika scanned the crowd, praying that nobody in the cast was among them.

When they got into the office, they had to wait because the manager was straightening out something in the electronics department. Then he came, fat and red in the face, and decided it was Erika who was the thief, but the security guard said no, she hadn't said or done anything as far as he could tell, just been there. The secretary called the police, who came right away. One of them knew Carrie from another arrest and said hi. The police took Erika's name and address and told her to go home, but not before she had turned around slowly to show she had nothing to hide.

With the keys clutched in her fist, she went outside and started looking for the car, but she couldn't remember which side of the mall they'd parked on. All of a sudden she realized how many white cars there were in the world.

By the time she found it, she had been around the outside of the mall two and a half times and decided for sure the car had been stolen. She was getting to like the idea, but then there it was, by light pole number 23, a white Saab convertible, double headlights, black leather seats and dash. She went over to it and got in behind the wheel.

She needed plenty of time, but she had plenty of time.

She went back inside the mall and called her father, asking him to pick her up at Carrie's dad's at six. Then she went back out to the lot, got in the car, put the key in the ignition, and started it so she was sure she'd be able to do it when she needed to. Then she turned it off and sat holding the wheel, deciding the exact route she would take through the lot to River Street.

She gave herself a pep talk. Pull yourself up by your own bootstraps, right? Except that this would be easier than that. Get out of the parking lot, stay in the right lane, and instead of making a left turn on Hudson Street, go past Hudson to the next street and make three right turns. Right? Right.

At five forty-five by the dashboard clock she started the

engine again, just to remind herself she knew how to do it. She found the lever that would pop the emergency break off, popping it a few times so she'd know how it sounded when it was completely off.

"Stay under fifteen," she said to herself. "Twenty if they beep at you. And don't practice. It won't help."

The part of the parking lot on the other side of Sears was almost completely empty, and the area in between wasn't busy except for one car, so now was the moment. She started up, put the car in drive, and went across the empty lot toward the River Street exit. Her idea was to time the traffic light so she'd be sure of getting out the exit without stopping or letting anybody see how young she was. She remembered it was an electric seat, which meant that maybe she could figure out how to lower it so she wouldn't stand out so much, but when she reached down there were three levers under there and she was afraid she'd move the one that made the seat higher.

A minivan with the right turn signal on got in front of her. She followed it. The light was yellow when she went through it, but that was all right. The thing to do was stay calm, follow her plan, keep to the right, and stay under fifteen. When she got past the mall, she had to stop and wait behind somebody who was leaving off passengers. All the cars behind her pulled out and drove around her. No problem. River Street had a lot more curves in it than she remembered, so for a second she wondered if she was still on it, but then came Mr. Ives's street, Hudson, and she went to the next road and made three right turns and she was on it. Soon, she was approaching his house. She pushed the garage door gizmo on the visor, made her first left turn into the driveway, drove the car into the garage, put the key behind the garden hose, and sat outside on the grass waiting for her father.

Erika and her dad went to Angelo's for dinner and got home at nine. Her father always went to bed early on Sunday so he could get to work early Monday. As soon as she heard him snoring, Erika took the phone into the bathroom, started the water, and dialed Jean's home number. Jean answered right away.

"Hello, Jean? If you're doing homework with your children, I can call back later."

"No. They're in bed. What is it?"

"Something's happened. I need to ask you a question. It has to do with my mom. My friend Carrie and I were at the mall today. And she got arrested for stealing."

"Just her? They let you go?"

"They took my name, and I gave them Mom's address."

"That's not something to worry about."

"I did break the law, but not until later, and nobody caught me."

"And nobody was injured?"

"No. I drove Carrie's dad's car. She gave me her father's keys when the security guy was taking us to the manager's office, and I drove it home for her."

"Her father's home?"

"Yes."

"And now it's there, and you're safe at home?"

"I'm at Dad's place."

"Dad's place, Erika, is where you've lived for four years and still live most of the time. If I was your dad, I would be happy if you saw it as one of your homes."

Erika said nothing.

"As your lawyer," Jean said, "I am bound to say that your action was very ill-advised."

"I didn't know what else to do."

"You have an attorney. In difficult circumstances, your attorney's job is to help you to consider your options. But you didn't call me to talk about that."

"I'm sorry."

"It's done, you're safe, we move on. What did Carrie take?"

"She took this $5.95 pair of pliers." There was a pause. "I could call you tomorrow in your office just as well if you have something else to do now."

"Erika, I am wide-awake and you have my complete attention."

"Okay. What I want to know is, if they find out Carrie

picked me up driving her father's car when I was home, would the judge hold it against Mom for letting me go with her?"

"Juvenile court and family court hardly ever talk to each other. They should, but they don't. So family court will never know it happened, and it would be a stretch to blame her anyway. Is that it?"

"Yes."

"Okay. Your attorney has some advice for you. Can you go in the bathroom without waking your father up?"

"That's where I am."

"I thought I heard an echo. Now I want you to put down the phone, take a few deep breaths, wash your face with cool water, and take a long, slow look in the mirror. You'll be looking at a smart, brave, beautiful young woman. Okay? Do it."

Erika put the phone down on a towel on the back of the toilet and washed her face and dried it and leaned into the mirror looking for pimples. Then she wiped her face with the towel again and went and picked up the phone. "I'm back."

"That was quick. Here's the second thing. The police might come to the house and ask you to write a statement. I want you ready for that, so before you go to sleep, take your diary and write down exactly what happened inside the mall while it's still fresh in your mind. Leave out the part about the car, which had nothing to do with Carrie's arrest. Write what happened inside the store, just the bare facts. Okay? And call me in the office tomorrow if you can."

"Okay."

"I know I've been hard on you in the last few minutes, but I want you to know, woman to woman, that you did very well today."

Erika started to cry.

"Cry, but don't hang up," Jean said.

After a minute, Erika got hold of herself. She put a cold washcloth across her eyes. "I trust you," she said.

"Thank you. I will not let you down. Now, get your report written and go to bed."

Dear Diary,

Here's what happened when Carrie and I went to Target in the mall. When we got to the Home Improvement Center, she picked up different tools and put them down again. She said she'd like to nail a ViceGrip to her father's bedroom wall in place of his crucifix to see how long it took him and his girlfriend to notice it. After a minute, the Security Guard stopped her and told us we were going to the Manager's office. When we got there we had to wait for him about ten minutes.

I had on my Levi's from last year and a tee shirt, so if I had stolen anything there would have been no way I could hide it, but he made me turn all the way around, so he could be sure, and empty my pockets. All I had was my wallet and two key rings. When the police came Carrie was very polite. I asked them if I could go with her to keep her company, but they told me I had to go home, which I did.

Done.

Erika

Locking her diary in her suitcase, she remembered what Carrie had said as they were walking through the Target entrance. She had grabbed her arm and whispered, "Risky business."

21

Halloween morning as she was getting ready for school, Erika looked over her shoulder at her father and said, "Carrie was arrested for stealing a pair of pliers at the mall yesterday. I was there. They took my name."

He reached for his coffee. "Is that all she stole?"

"That's all."

"Everybody knows she's a criminal."

"I don't know that."

"Then you're not seeing straight."

"Anyway, I just wanted you to know."

"She didn't put the blame on you?"

"She wouldn't do something like that."

"Yes, she would. Then she'd make up some bogus reason

to think it was the right thing to do. I never said she was stupid, just bad."

"Well, I better get to school. Rehearsal today."

"Fine."

Carrie didn't come to school. Erika called her when she got home. She sounded very happy.

"Larry the Loser's on the case. I'm not going back to school ever."

22

Halloween night, after her kids were back from trick-or-treating, Jean drove into town to drop in at Mr. Nevski's apartment. Erika opened the door a few inches and then stepped sideways and opened it wider. Her legs were tied at the ankles. "I have to walk in a narrow skirt in the play," she said. "I've been handing out candy all night like this. Mr. Stork said I should do this to get used to it."

"Does it help?"

Erika shrugged her shoulders. "I've only fallen down once." She led the way slowly into the living room and sat down on the couch and began to untie herself.

Mr. Nevski waved his hand at the new TV. "That's the set I was telling you Erika needed," he said. "She loves it. Also, I worked out a better cable connection." He looked at Erika.

"You were amazed, right? We're watching hockey. I used to play."

Erika finished untying her second ankle and stood up. "Dad was a semipro," she said. She went into the kitchen to make coffee. Jean and Mr. Nevski sat and talked about the weather, sports injuries, and how instant replay changed the way people watched games. Only when the conversation petered out did he turn the TV off. "What can I show you? Anything?"

Jean leaned back. "I'd like to see the rest of your apartment before I leave, but I'm in no hurry."

Erika came in with the coffee and some birthday cake she'd saved in the freezer for Jean's visit. Mr. Nevski told Jean about the game in which his nose was broken, which had cured his allergies but made food taste bad for a long time. Jean thought about her family. At this moment her husband would be listening to Nathan practice his trumpet in the basement, Christa would be getting ready for bed, and Martin, who always seemed to have a pile of homework, would be bent over the dining room table doing it. She wanted to be there.

She asked Erika if the visit was keeping her from homework, and even though she usually did it in the kitchen, Erika brought Jean to her room so she could see the desk she worked at sometimes. Mr. Nevski came after them and showed Jean how good the desk light was by turning it on and off, and made Jean sit on the chair to see how perfect it was. "You see," he said. "It's soft, but not so cushy she'd fall asleep in it. I got it from work. They gave the whole sales force new desks, new chairs, everything."

On the way to the front door, Mr. Nevski told Jean how glad he was that Erika had a lawyer to speak up for her.

"I just want you to know," he said, holding the door open, "I'm a reasonable man, and whatever the judge decides is okay with me, as long as it's in the best interests of my daughter, which if he decides just on the basis of what's right it will be."

Dear Diary,

Jean was here tonight. After she left, Daddy said there was no justice for working people because all the judges and half the lawyers went to Yale or Harvard and they didn't know what it was to work and still be poor. He also said if the judge gives me to Mom he'll fight it all the way up to the Supreme Court. Then when he was in the bathroom shaving I heard him crying. When he came out with his face all red I had to walk him to bed and bring him a glass of water and tell him I knew he'd fight. I don't want to talk about it.

Stork says Frank and I won't kiss at all until dress rehearsal. He's afraid everybody's going to go wild when we do, which is a pretty old-fashioned idea. It's complicated because John and Kate aren't truly in love, so they kiss like they're strangers even though they're engaged. He wants me to look stiff when we do it, and count 1, 2, 3 and then pull my head back. I don't want to practice kissing Frank like I didn't love him. Then he says he's going to figure out some way for Frank and me to "get familiar." MEANING?????

If I don't get better remembering lines, I'm going to ruin it for everybody, like that kid Hughie.

Love,

Erika

23

Jean was in the middle of frying up hamburgers for dinner Wednesday evening when the phone rang. It was Erika's father.

"There was this detective here just now," he said. "I told you about Carrie, right, Erika's so-called friend? Well, she stole a pair of pliers at the mall with Erika there. What do you think about that?"

"I've discussed it with her, and I'm fairly sure she's not in serious trouble with the police. I tell you this because I know you worry about her and she would want me to try to relieve your mind."

"Well, you don't know the worst. This detective wanted to talk to Erika about what happened. She's over at the library, but I didn't tell him that. He said Carrie told the police somebody named Bonnie had taken the pliers and put them in her pocket so she'd be blamed, so they think maybe Erika's Bonnie, when really Bonnie's this make-believe girl Carrie used to pretend was telling her to do things just to drive her mom crazy. So anyway, you'll handle this, right?"

Jean turned off the burner under the frying pan. "Can you hold on a minute, please?" She put the phone on the top of the refrigerator, picked up the frying pan, went over to the table, got the burgers onto the plates, called to her husband and kids to come eat, and took the phone into the laundry room.

"We don't know yet if there's anything that needs to be handled," she said.

"She's got to have somebody for this."

"The Children's Law Center works in family court. I have no experience with juvenile court. In my view, it is very unlikely that Erika will have to deal with criminal charges. If it turns out she needs someone, I'll see to it."

"It's got to be you. Nobody can trust two lawyers. And another thing, just so you know. She didn't go to the mall from my house. She was over at my ex's when Carrie picked her up, which was in a stolen car, which the bitch knew, or should have, and she let her go anyway."

"My understanding is that it was Carrie's father's car."

"Did her father know she had it? Answer me that. Never mind. I hear Erika coming up the stairs. You can talk to her."

"No. This is your phone call, Mr. Nevski, not hers or

mine. I have no reason at this moment to talk to her. It's dinnertime, and I have to sit down with my family and eat. Tell her what happened. If she wants to talk to me, she'll call."

"Just get on for ten seconds and tell her to drop Carrie."

"I'm not going to do that now or ever, Mr. Nevski. Carrie is her friend. Carrie stood by her when all the other kids in Mrs. Droste's class turned away."

There was silence at the other end.

"Are you still there, Mr. Nevski?"

"Yeah, I'm here. How'd you know?"

"I'm going to tell you a story now, and then I'm going to say goodbye. My father's best friend in high school was a boy named Tommy. Senior year, Tommy started stealing cars. My father stayed friends with him. When Tommy was arrested and sentenced to three months, my father was in the courtroom. When Tommy got out, my father helped him get a job. When people asked him why he didn't drop Tommy, my dad said, 'If Jesus didn't drop Judas, who he knew was going to betray him, why should I drop Tommy, when all he did was steal cars?' End of story."

"Okay. Just one more thing. Did you and Erika have a fight or something? Is that why you want to bring some other lawyer in? Not that I care, as long as he isn't Carrie's."

"May I give you some advice, Mr. Nevski?"

"What?"

"Your beautiful daughter, who has never had a part in a play, has a starring role in a play opening two weeks from tomorrow. It will not help her to listen to you knocking her friends."

"You're wrong."

Jean said nothing.

"You still there?"

"Yes."

"Well, you're wrong. She was in a play in second grade. She was some kind of vegetable."

Jean took a deep breath. "I'm going to say goodbye now, Mr. Nevski. Goodbye."

24

Thursday, when everybody was just goofing around waiting for the Stork to finish talking to the lighting crew, Mrs. Fine took Erika into the dressing room and had her put on all four costumes she'd gotten together for her. Erika didn't want to say anything, because Mrs. Fine seemed satisfied, but when she put on the city suit for the first scene of the second act, she thought it didn't look like something Kate would go downtown in.

"I probably won't, but if I go to the Salvation Army and see something, could I bring it in and see what you think?"

"I didn't think you cared all that much how you looked. I'm glad," Mrs. Fine said. "Absolutely, yes. A fitted jacket and a narrow, dark green party skirt, that's what I'd look for. Green's your color."

At the end of rehearsal, the Stork sat everybody down on the edge of the stage. "Fourteen days," he said. "Three hundred and thirty-six hours." He smiled and made his eyes big. "Just a reminder, cast. Everybody take five except Frank and Erika."

He led the pair out through the auditorium doors into the hall. "You guys are both too stiff when you're together," he said. "I have this friend who's a salesman at Verne's. In the mall. Mr. Lemons. He was a Footlighter ten years ago. I want you to go there Saturday or Sunday and pick out a wedding ring. Go in and ask for Mr. Lemons. I already talked to him. He knows you're coming. Tell him you're John and Kate and you want a wedding ring." He looked at Erika. "Just for you. This is 1910 in England. Men didn't wear wedding rings. Okay? That's your assignment."

He went back in the auditorium.

The two of them looked at each other.

"I don't want to do that," Frank said.

Erika lied. "Neither do I," she said. It would be the first thing she had ever done in her life that Carrie would be jealous of.

Frank shook his head. "Acting onstage is one thing. The mall's the real world."

When they went back in the auditorium, the rest of the cast was doing the scene where the mother accuses the father of keeping on with the case just for personal glory. She and Frank sat with Sonia in the third row watching, and when it was over and everybody was getting ready to go, Frank said to her, "Sonia thinks it'd be fun, and we sort of acted like we were going to do it, so it's okay with me if it's okay with you. I work tomorrow, but Sunday would be fine. I could meet you at twelve. Something like that. What do you think?"

"Sure."

She and Sonia left the building together. Mrs. Ives was waiting in her car at the curb. Halfway there, Erika stopped Sonia. "Can I ask you something? Stork said Frank and I are stiff, which I guess we are. Do you think Frank doesn't like me?"

"He thinks you're great. It's the Stork's fault. With two weeks to go, he should start letting you kiss in rehearsal. He has you go through all the motions, including leaning back and lifting your leg, which looks stupid if you're not kissing somebody, and then he stops you."

25

Sunday, Erika left her mom's early and took the bus to the mall. At eleven forty-five she was walking back and forth between the entrance to Target and the top of the escalator, looking at stuff in store windows and reading signs. At twelve she saw Frank and Sonia coming up. Sonia smiled and gave a little wave. Frank had gotten another haircut. He was almost bald. As soon as the two of them got off the escalator, they all started walking toward the jewelry store. When it came in sight, they stopped.

"Frank called me last night, and asked me to come," Sonia said. "I called your mom's to tell you, but there was no answer."

Frank looked at Erika and smiled. "You still feel like doing it?"

"Why not?" Erika said. "You?"

"Sure. But fast. In and out and we're done."

"Right."

"Let's go," Frank said, and began to march toward Verne's, which was two stores past Sears. Erika caught up with him as he was walking in the door, and they went to the ring counter together. A man with a tan jacket, a white shirt, and a narrow bow tie came over.

"May I help you?"

"Mr. Stork said we should ask for Mr. Lemons," Frank said.

"At your service," Mr. Lemons said. "I thought you wouldn't be coming during the lunch hour, but this is fine. Let me show you our wedding rings. Nothing but the best for the best." He slid open the back of the case, pulled out two black velvet trays of rings, and laid them carefully on the counter.

Erika pointed to one, a narrow silver circle with seven small diamonds. "That one," she said.

Mr. Lemons took it out and laid it on a black velvet square. "That's very nice," he said, "but I have time. You don't have to hurry. There are others you might find more to your taste."

"No, that's the one," Erika said. "Really. Thanks. It's the prettiest one there." She stepped back to go.

Mr. Lemons looked at Frank. "Sir, will you want to try it out on her, see how it looks on her finger?"

"It's bad luck," Frank said, and the two of them left with the ring still on the counter.

"That was quick," Sonia said when they got out the door.

"She knew what she wanted," Frank said, and as they walked away he squeezed Erika's arm and said, "Thanks. That was great."

She thought, for a second, of trying on bridal gowns, but there was no way she could do that. They went to the food court and had lunch.

As they were eating, Frank took a flashlight out of his pocket. "I found it backstage yesterday. See, it's got your name on the tape. The batteries still work." He pointed it at Erika and turned it on and off three times.

"Thanks."

"I put it in the back of the panel the night of dress rehearsal for *Birdie*. Remember? You were up on the spotlight platform and I was standing right under you."

Erika felt herself blushing.

"I was holding on to you," he said. "Did you mind?"

"No, it was okay," she said, getting up and putting the flashlight in her backpack.

On their way to the exit, Sonia came up behind Frank and pushed him into Erika, and the three of them bounced off each other until they got to the mall entrance and said goodbye.

Dear Diary,

If I ever get married, which I probably won't, we're going to make our own wedding rings. No diamonds, no pearls, no rubies, no built-in TV set. We'll go out in the woods and find some vines twirling around some tree, no start and no finish, and we'll copy them. Which means I'll have to learn how to make jewelry. Why not? Maybe we'll live in a log cabin in the woods like the family on your cover. Although I'd rather chop trees than do laundry.

26

When she was back from the mall, Erika called Carrie to see how she was doing.

"Why didn't you call before?" Carrie asked. "I need you here tonight."

Erika could tell from her voice that she was serious. "I'll call and ask my dad," she said.

"Tell him you're staying at your mom's one more night. He hates her, so he won't call to find out if you're there. Then let your mom think you're at your dad's, and we'll come pick you up at the end of Ulster Street at five."

Erika dialed her father's number. "Dad, it's really important. I've got to go to Carrie's tonight. I'll go to school from there. Okay?"

"Go ahead," he said. "Why should I get between you and your own private Judas?"

"What do you mean?"

"Ask your lawyer."

That night, Mrs. Ives cooked strip steak and peppers, which was her daughter's favorite. Right after dinner they went up to Carrie's room.

"Remember I mentioned you could make the play better and you said you didn't want to?" Carrie asked. "Well, think about this. Just think about it. In act two, where the lawyer gives her brother a hard time and calls him a thief, what you should do is look straight out at the audience and say, 'That's shitty.' "

"Kate would never say that," Erika said.

"Right, but put yourself in her place. You might if you were really pissed off. I don't mean do it in rehearsals. You save it until the last night of the show. Everybody will remember you. Nobody will ever forget it as long as the school's there. If the Stork goes to some other school, the story will go there with him. You're going to be at Fillmore next year anyway. Why not do something people are going to remember when you're gone? There'll be this stunned silence. You don't like the guy who's playing the lawyer anyway, so he blows his line and it's chaos, but you've made your point."

"I don't know my lines well enough to think about changing them."

Carrie shrugged her shoulders. "Okay. Forget it. I'm just trying to lift you up a little above the crowd. Let's look at a movie."

She had a shelf next to her TV with fifty-seven DVDs. Her favorite was *Girl, Interrupted*, all except the last ten minutes, when Winona Ryder gets sane again and leaves the nuthouse to take a part-time job in a bookstore. It was the third time seeing it for Erika, but she liked Winona Ryder.

"If I ever get put in a nuthouse and after a while start to get less crazy, I hope I'm smart and strong enough to make them let me out."

"It's saner inside than outside," Carrie said. "Only crazy people really know how to live."

Around 2:00 a.m. they got in their beds and turned out the lights and Carrie said she had another idea about the play that didn't mean changing any lines. Erika should cut her hair the day of opening night and just show up that way. "Match Frank. Be twinsies. It's what you really want in real life anyway."

Erika didn't say anything.

Carrie turned on her light again. "Feel under your pillow. Reach under there. Take a look. It's for your birthday."

Erika reached under her pillow and pulled out a brown envelope with the courthouse name printed in the upper-left-hand corner.

"It's the court record of your parents' divorce. Citizens have a right to know what's going on in their court system.

Did you know that? It's part of living in a great democracy. Mom asked me what she could do for me, and I asked her to go get it, and she did. She does what I tell her. She's truly crazy. She went to the central record office or whatever it is. She had to be checked for knives and guns and then stand around waiting for a long time, because the senior clerk had to tell some junior clerk to go in the basement or somewhere and get it, but then they gave it to her. Sold it to her. One fifty a page, but a really good print job. She didn't read it, but I did. A lot of legal stuff, boring, but what your mom told the judge about your dad makes interesting reading. Open it up and look. They're ready to kill each other over you. You're on thirteen, fifteen, and thirty-seven. The best is what they say about each other. You could look at it and swear out a warrant or something saying what's true and what's not. What you knew about, anyway. I should have asked her to get me a copy of hers and Daddy's. I wonder if she would have. Why not? Or don't swear out a warrant and your parents would never know."

Erika turned the corner of the envelope up. "It's thick."

"I marked the parts where they accuse each other of stuff. Your lawyer's probably read it, so why shouldn't you?"

Erika swung herself around on the bed and stuffed it back under her pillow.

"Happy birthday. Bedtime reading. Like Stephen King, but with monsters you know."

Carrie came over to Erika's bed, sat down, and leaned forward so she was looking directly in Erika's eyes.

"They're sending me away. I don't care. You're not telling me, but you know all about it, right?"

Erika's heart fell. "No. I don't," she said.

"You can tell me. Mom tells you everything, so you must know. A school for the criminal children of rich parents. It's deep in the woods of Wisconsin. Maybe they don't have any woods. Whatever. Prairies. Mountains. The only way they'd not send me would be if Larry the Loser came up with some other deal to send me twice as far away. There'll be some really interesting kids there. They'll hate me."

"No they won't," Erika said.

"Yes they will," Carrie said. "It's how I want it. I can hardly wait to get there."

"You want to go? Really?"

"It's a done deal. I don't care as long as the food's good and as long as you're going to miss me. I want to know that there's somebody back East who knows that nobody can take my place. Larry's cooked it all up. I'm not guessing. I know. If I go, there's some stuff of mine I want to give you." She got off the bed and went to her dresser and took a tape recorder out of the bottom drawer. "The evidence," she said, waggling it in the air. "You can order these spy devices on the Internet, so I'm not just guessing what Larry's up to. I know. I've got his words right here." She put the tape recorder back in the drawer. "How much does Miss Jean make?"

"Who?"

"Your lawyer. From the Kiddie Law Factory. Dad and Mom must pay Larry five or ten times more than she gets. Like three hundred dollars an hour or something. You look like you got an itch. You want some Benadryl?"

"No, thanks."

Carrie got back in her bed. She always fell asleep fast. Erika rolled over onto her stomach and thought about her first year with Dad, saving up money, planning to hitchhike to Arizona so her mom would want to either come back or keep her there. That was when she started to wonder if the whole world was a dream you never woke up from. In the dark it made a lot of sense. When Daddy had the TV on it was worse, because she knew no matter how real the people talking sounded, they were dreams, in a way. The only cure when she began to feel dizzy was to get up, sneak through the kitchen, go downstairs to the front stoop, and stand there taking deep breaths and smelling the different smells and watching the traffic light on Franklin Street changing from red to green and back again, and the cars starting and stopping, and saying to herself over and over again, "The cars are real and the people in them are real and the whole world is real." Then she could go back and go to sleep.

She reached under the covers and grabbed her right ankle and held it tight, the way Frank had.

27

The next morning, Erika woke up and opened her eyes. Mrs. Ives was there with her finger to her lips. "We'll let Carrie sleep," she whispered. "Come on downstairs. Breakfast is ready and we have a lot to do."

Erika looked at the clock. It was five-thirty.

"I need to ask you some things," Mrs. Ives said.

When they were downstairs she put a plate of toast and bacon and scrambled eggs on the kitchen table. "As you know, Carrie's going to Wisconsin today," she said.

Erika's heart fell again. "I didn't know that," she said.

"Didn't she tell you last night? Maybe you were half asleep when she said it."

Erika shook her head. "I don't think so. No."

"Our attorney worked it all out," Mrs. Ives said. "They

had a juvenile court hearing Friday and he reached an agreement with the judge, so instead of juvenile detention she's going to a school where they have girls who've been in a little trouble. She'll have regular school plus treatment. It's a wonderful place." She got her big leather purse, took out a color brochure for the Plains Opportunity School, and put it next to Erika's plate. "This tells all about it."

On the front cover was a photograph of some big white houses with bushes and flowers and trees. Behind them was a red barn and a fenced area full of cows. Each page of the brochure had a title: "Starting Out," with pictures of kids getting out of vans in front of the houses, sitting at their desks in their dorms, and standing around a campfire singing. "Sorting Out," with two pictures of kids sitting in classrooms paying close attention to their teachers, plus one picture of a girl talking to a friendly man in a tweed jacket. "Working Out," with kids driving tractors, picking what looked like blueberries from high bushes, and putting on a play in costume. And "Setting Out," with graduation day pictures of happy students, teachers, and parents.

The last page was an application form.

Erika handed the brochure back. Mrs. Ives looked directly in her eyes. Erika knew what was coming. "How does it look to you?"

"Great."

"They have horses. The kids go riding, those who want, even in the winter. It's very outdoorsy, which is healthy. Did you see the picture of them putting on a play? Small classes, eight to twelve. And they place them in good colleges when they graduate, not just Wisconsin colleges, not that there's anything wrong with them. Doesn't it make you sad to think of Carrie going and you being left behind here? Plains isn't just for kids who've been in trouble. Mainly it's for kids who are just fine the way they are, but their parents both know they could become even better in the right atmosphere. And it's not just for kids with parents who can afford it. They give scholarships. So might a place like that interest you? It's a family there, not just a mom in one house and a dad in the other and never the twain shall meet. Everybody working together."

"It's good she got in," Erika said.

"Would you like to go there with her? When the play's over, naturally. Carrie's father and I would pay. We both know how close you two are. And, speaking frankly, I'd be a lot happier with you there to remind her about staying on the straight and narrow path. Of course I'll miss you, but Carrie has first claim on you, and there are long weekends you can fly home. What do you think?"

Erika hated to have to say no to people. "I don't think so," she said.

Mrs. Ives reached across the table and patted her shoulder. "It's all right, you don't have to go. It was just an idea. Everybody thinks Carrie's a bad girl and you know she isn't, and I just thought it would be nice for her to have somebody like that there. She'll win a lot of friends, of course, but none as good as you."

"What you're doing is really a good thing," Erika said.

Mrs. Ives poured herself a cup of coffee. "Can I tell you what I thought after the incident at the mall? I thought that maybe, just maybe, you were the one who did the stealing and Carrie was protecting you by taking the blame. Especially since she told the police that Bonnie had done it. You remember her make-believe friend she used to talk to in the back of the car? And I said to myself, Maybe when she says Bonnie she really means Erika. She was so lighthearted about it, and it was just the two of you there. That's right, isn't it?"

Erika nodded her head.

"That's what I thought. It's so crazy. She had her father's credit card, which he lets her use. Why steal something? Really, I'm asking you. If you don't know why, who would?"

Erika didn't answer.

"She did it for a joke," Mrs. Ives said. "That's what it was. A childish prank. Did she take her father's car? He told me it wasn't parked in the garage just the way he left it. Maybe some friend drove it home for her."

"I was the one who did that."

A look of admiration came into Mrs. Ives's face. "Really?" She put her hand on Erika's shoulder. "Don't ever let her father know. You don't mind that I asked you to go away with her, do you?"

"No," Erika said. "Really. It's nice of you to offer."

"Actually, I'd miss you almost as much as I'm going to miss Carrie. Anyway, I want you to go to the airport with her. She says she'll run away if I try to drive her there. The plane leaves at eleven-eighteen, but you know these days you have to be there hours and hours ahead. You'll have plenty of time when you're finished to go to school. You won't miss a second of rehearsal. Okay?"

Erika wanted to say no, but she couldn't, not to her best friend's mom.

"Airports aren't like they used to be. You have to get there early and then you say goodbye and the person goes through security an hour ahead. The people from Plains Opportunity are going to drive down to meet her, but Carrie's got to get on the plane here, so after you say goodbye I want you to wait and make sure she doesn't come out. Will you do that? The taxi will wait for you and bring you to school. It will work out fine. There's something else, too. She may want to give you some jewelry to hold for her. The only trouble is, it's not her jewelry to give. It's from her grandmother. She's probably shown it to you."

"I don't think so," Erika said.

Mrs. Ives smiled. "You've just forgotten. Legally and morally, all that jewelry is mine. So don't let her give you anything, okay?"

Erika and Carrie were in a taxi on the way to the airport. Mrs. Ives had given the driver a fifty-dollar bill to go there, and Erika a second fifty-dollar bill to get a cab to school. As soon as they were out of sight of her house, Carrie took a small cardboard box covered with duct tape out of her pocket. "I want you to keep this for me," she said.

Erika shook her head. "I shouldn't."

"Why not?" Carrie asked. "It isn't weed, if that's what you think. My experiment was a failure. All I could get to grow in Daddy's basement was little stems."

"I didn't think that," Erika said.

"Then you think it's my grandmother's jewelry, which she gave to me before she died. I know. My mom thinks it's still hers. Okay, forget it." She put the box back in her pocket.

They talked about stealing, how it felt to drive a car in traffic for the first time, and how terrible it was to marry the wrong person, and then they were getting out of the cab at the airport.

Carrie pulled the divorce transcript from under her coat and stuffed it in Erika's backpack. "You left it under your pillow," she said.

When they got near the security gate, they hugged each other. Erika wanted to cry, but she couldn't.

"Stay with me until I get through the metal detector, and then go," Carrie said. "I promise I'll get on the plane."

Erika didn't promise to stay until the plane took off. They got into the line. When they reached the woman who was checking tickets, Carrie pulled the box out of her pocket, pushed it into Erika's hand, and stepped away. "It's a test of your trust. Keep it someplace safe and you pass."

Erika hung around until Carrie was past security and then left the terminal. Near the taxicab stand she took off her backpack, put Carrie's box in it, took the divorce transcript out, and dropped it in a trash can. It made a bang hitting the bottom. The cab was waiting. She told the driver to go to Orchard Street.

Jean was in court, but Kit and Oz were there.

"He's had a bad morning," Kit said. "He just came from the vet. His dog was hit by a car. Go in and see him. Cheer him up."

Erika went to his office. He was sitting behind his desk picking up papers and putting them down again. She waited.

He looked up. "Hi."

"Are you busy?"

"No." He turned the picture of his dog toward her. "You never met Rolph. He ran into the side of a car this morning. I was taking him for a walk and I didn't have a tight hold on his leash and he saw this squirrel or bunny rabbit or something across the road and went after him. He's okay, but he broke two ribs. I know what it is to have broken ribs. Every time you breathe it hurts. As soon as he's all healed up, we're going to go to dog obedience classes. They have them at your school once a year in the spring. He's going to be okay. That's what I have to remember. So, what's new with you?"

"I just said goodbye to my best friend."

His phone rang. Erika went out to the waiting room and asked Kit when she thought Jean would be back.

"Fifteen minutes? A half hour?" Kit said.

Erika knew from the picture on Oz's desk what Rolph looked like—long nose, big brown eyes with something like furry eyebrows over them, curly brown fur, pointy ears—so she went in the old safe and got a piece of construction paper and folded it like a card. Then in her backpack she found her old set of colored pens, which hadn't dried out, and drew a ball of fur in one corner, a nose in the middle, a big brown eye with a black eyebrow, and two ears, and inside she wrote, "Dear Rolph, I hope you're all put together again soon to take Oz for walks. Love, Erika."

She put it in Oz's mailbox over Kit's desk.

Jean came in and didn't seem surprised to find Erika waiting for her. She invited her into her office. Oz came out and trailed along.

As soon as they were settled, Erika took the package out.

"My friend Carrie gave it to me last thing before she went to Wisconsin this morning. Could I leave it here overnight?"

Jean sat down. "Carrie's the one who stole the pliers?"

"Yes."

"Do you know if what's in the box really belongs to her?"

"You think I should open it and make sure?" Erika asked.

Jean smiled. "It's up to you."

Erika sat down at the table and started working on it. Her hands felt jumpy. Finally she got all the tape off and opened the lid. Inside, wrapped in Kleenex, was the Little Miss Muffet figurine from Carrie's dresser. There was a note in a little envelope.

Dear Erika, If you trusted me, you wouldn't be reading this, so I guess you lose.

Erika felt ashamed of herself. She handed the note to Jean.

"She wants to own you," Jean said.

Erika put the figurine back in the box and sat staring at it. "I should have trusted her. She's my best friend."

"In fifth grade she was," Jean said. "Not now. Now she wants to punish you."

"She has," Erika said, and started to cry. Jean came around behind her and put her hands on her shoulders. Erika pushed the lid back on the box and put it in Jean's hands. "I have to get Carrie's address from her mom and send it to her. Can you keep it here for a while?"

"For as long as you want."

Erika went down the hall to the bathroom and washed her face, came back, and stood in the doorway. "I better get to school. I've got a taxi waiting, all paid for."

"I'll call you this afternoon after rehearsal," Jean said. "Will you be home?"

"You don't need to do that," Erika said. "Really, I'm fine. I'm just glad there wasn't anything in the package I'd have to call her mother about."

Jean and Oz both hugged her, and she left.

Jean and Oz went to the window. Kit came in and stood with them. They watched Erika walk down the stairs and stand at the curb looking at the playground across the street.

"Erika looked completely beat going out the door," Kit said. "Why did you let her go that way? I wouldn't trust her to cross a street by herself. What happened?"

"Her best friend just slapped her in the face," Oz said.

"So you're just going to stand there and watch her go? Take her to the movies. Take her shopping. Don't leave her alone."

Jean grabbed her coat.

During lunch at a coffee shop, Erika talked about her city clothes in the play. She still didn't like them. When lunch was over, they went to the Salvation Army store. Inside, Jean led the way over to an old lady putting men's pants on hangers. "Excuse me, this is my sister Erika. She's an actress, and she's searching for something very particular."

The woman looked up and smiled. "What can I do for you?"

"Erika is a working woman in London a hundred years ago. You know, she goes out to get votes for women, so she has to look rich and nice. If we could find the exact right skirt, dark green, and perhaps one or two jackets, and we'll need the right blouse. Not fussy. Formal."

They looked and looked, and finally chose a cream blouse and a long skirt, but no jacket. "We can't leave without the one perfect jacket," Jean said.

The old lady's eyes lit up. "I know. There's a tuxedo from an all-girl symphony orchestra in the storage area. We don't have any call for something like that, but it's silk and in perfect condition, so we can't throw it away, either. We're not supposed to take customers there, but this seems like a special case."

She led them through a swinging door and around some long tables to an alcove in the back, pushed aside a curtain, ran her hand down a rack of tuxedos, pulled one out, and held it up. "There's a dickey somewhere. I just need to find it."

"What's a dickey?" Erika asked.

The lady pulled something stiff and white out of a box. "You clip it around your neck. It's just a collar and a front. It'll go right over your T-shirt. You won't need the vest. Put your long green skirt on under it and you'll be able to go anywhere."

Erika put the jacket on. It fit perfectly. She started to go over to the mirror.

"No!" Jean said. "Let me pin your hair up first." She took a comb and some pins out of her pocket and did the job in half a minute. Then she pushed Erika to the mirror and stood behind her. It was amazing. From the hips down she was Erika, and from the hips up she was a London lady.

Jean drove her to school, said goodbye, went to the guidance office to get her absence excused, and drove to her office.

Erika brought the new things to the costume room and showed them to Mrs. Fine, who said they were perfect.

Rehearsal was beginning. Erika started along the crowded space between the back curtain and the rear wall of the stage, walking around chairs and old pieces of scenery, she met Frank coming the other way.

"The Stork is losing it," he said.

"How do you know?"

"His eyes are bugging out. Really. You'll see."

The rehearsal ran until six, and it was all screaming.

When it was over, Erika decided to go to the library and study her lines there. She'd done it a few times before. It was the perfect place, four blocks from her dad's apartment with well-lighted streets in between, and quiet; the whole library was carpeted so you could walk around and not make any noise. Also, the reference room had an English look, with high windows, lots of little panes, books along the walls, and even a couple of big vases on the wide windowsill of the center window.

It was the short lines that worried Erika the most. So many of them were alike, and if she gave the wrong one she'd throw the other actor off. Unless it was Frank. Frank knew what your line was supposed to be and just went straight on as if you'd said it.

When she got to the library, instead of turning right toward the reference room she turned left to the children's library and sat on the floor in the corner reading all the Petunia the Silly Goose books. They had four. As long as she was looking at the pictures she didn't feel any panic at all, but as soon as she closed one her heart would start to pound and it would keep up until she was into the next book. She thought about the children who had skipped Petunia and taken out other books, and she thanked them in her heart for leaving the Petunia books for her.

When she got back to her dad's, Karen sat in the living room yelling at him for abandoning her, giving her asthma, and ruining her life, while he yelled back that she and the bitch together had ruined his, and Erika lay on her bed knowing she was going to ruin the play. She knew most of her lines, but there were some scenes, including the first one, where she was forgetting lines and saying others at the wrong time. Finally she threw the script on the floor and kicked it under the bed. At eleven-thirty she heard the door slam and knew that Karen was gone.

Wednesday Erika went to the library to work, and when she got home Karen was sitting with her dad watching TV.

Erika went in and sat with them, but in a minute Karen started saying the same things she had said the night before and Erika ran to the bathroom and turned on the water to drown out the noise. Thursday, with Erika's dad at work, Karen came and talked to Erika until he came in, and then started yelling, and Friday she showed up at the pizza place and sat down and told them in a low voice how miserable she was.

When Erika went home Saturday, Karen apologized and told her that she was a completely new person. She was going to go back to school and end up at the top of her class.

"I've got everything under control," she said. "Also, I'm working out every day starting tomorrow, or maybe Monday."

Erika realized Karen was high on something. "Are you okay?" she asked.

"What do you mean am I okay? You think because you're a star you can decide there's something wrong with me?"

"No," Erika said. "Really not. I was just asking."

Karen said something so softly Erika couldn't understand it.

"What'd you say?" Erika asked. "I missed it."

"Too bad for you, then," Karen said. "I don't have to talk to people who aren't listening to begin with. Where's your head? What are you doing?"

"Trying to remember all my lines. It's dress rehearsal Wednesday."

"You haven't learned them yet? They should have given me the part. Bernie and I are going somewhere. Remember what I said when you went with Daddy and I stayed with Mom? I said I was old enough to be your aunt but I was always going to be your sister. Well I always kept my promise, right? You remember?"

"Sure," Erika said, ashamed to be telling a lie.

That night, she dreamed again of her mom's place full of fire.

28

Erika sat up in bed. What day was it? Thursday? No. Wednesday. Still dark. She could go back to sleep. Good.

She went to the bathroom. Sitting on the toilet, she pressed her feet onto the cold tiles, and when she stood up she stepped onto a spot next to the window where it was cool again. She looked out. There was a little snowstorm going on. Watching the snowflakes fly by the streetlamp made her dizzy. She washed her face with cold water and went back to bed. She imagined the Stork calling her to his office and telling her Sonia knew all Kate's lines so he was giving her the part. The idea made her feel sick to her stomach. She went to her backpack and felt around in the bottom. At first she couldn't find the bottle of Accudane Bernie had given her back in October, but then she did. She'd have to take it out before going to school, if she remembered.

Later that morning, when she put her backpack in her locker, the Accudane was still in it. In homeroom, the morning announcements included the fact that tickets were still available for the Thursday and Friday night performances of *The Winslow Boy*. Saturday was sold out. That was the night Jean was coming.

Dress rehearsal was supposed to begin at six-thirty. At six-fifteen, with her first-act dress on and her makeup done, Erika left the auditorium and walked down the hall toward her locker. Halfway there she passed Mr. Dillon, the custodian, pushing a broom. It felt strange. Here she was dressed like a London woman of a hundred years ago and he didn't even look at her. She took her backpack out of her locker, opened it, and got out the bottle of pills.

"Bernie's right about one thing," she said as she unscrewed the lid. "You should only take medications that make you more true to yourself, or something like that."

She put two pills in her mouth, the minimum dose according to Bernie, and chewed them. They tasted like vinegar. They even smelled like vinegar. Halfway back to the auditorium, with Mr. Dillon now at the far end of the hall, she turned and went back to her locker and took one more, which was still less than what Bernie had said was an okay amount.

A group of people came down the east stairway, and for a second Erika thought they had come to watch the dress rehearsal, but then she saw they were all carrying books, so they were probably students in some adult education class. She went back through the door to the stage and stood next to Sonia. Lucky Sonia—no costume changes, lots to do but not many lines, and at the end a long speech telling everyone what had happened in the courtroom.

"You're going to be fine," Sonia said. "You're going to hit all the marks."

"So are you."

Erika suddenly felt hot. She walked over to the corner behind the light panel and looked for the script she had left there. It was gone. "I don't need it, I know my lines," she said to herself, but she kept looking and reaching behind things. She wanted it to be last year, when she was stage crew.

The Stork jumped onto the stage and called everybody together, but Erika stayed where she was. She wondered why he never combed his hair down but let it fly all over the place. He asked for a show of hands. How many kids had sold over seventy-five tickets? No hands. Fifty? Still no hands. Thirty? Sonia put her hand halfway up. He started applauding, and everybody joined in. The marching band, he said, had sold fifty. Who had sold tickets to at least five people not in their families? Eight or ten hands went up. Erika looked around for Frank in his army uniform. He was probably still in the boys' dressing room. There was a girl standing beside her she'd never seen before. What was she, the curtain puller's girlfriend?

Erika's father used to talk about Carl Yastrzemski, the Red Sox player whose eye on the ball was so sharp it slowed the ball down on its way, coming to him foot by foot and inch by inch so when it got to where he wanted it he could nail it. Erika's ears were that way now. Each word the Stork said was clear and separate from every other word. He started going over the rules. Enter on cue. Pay attention to what everyone else is saying. Relax. Don't make noise backstage. Don't depend on the mikes.

Her legs felt tired, and she had a pain in her stomach. The Stork started yelling at Pat Mulhall, who was sitting at the P.A. system panel. Why couldn't he get the mikes to work? The Stork went over and looked at the dials, about which he knew nothing. The curtains started to open, and then closed fast. Somebody bumped into Erika. The Stork yelled "Ready!" and then "Curtain!" and she walked out into the lights and spoke her opening line:

A problem in ethics for you, Father.

As the scene went on Erika began watching the seat in the middle of the front row where her mom would need to sit so she could get all the action and hear all the lines. The moment came for her first long speech. She walked to the edge of the stage and said as clearly and politely as she could:

My mom needs to be sitting in that middle seat right there, so you have to have somebody save it for her.

The sound system began to whistle. Then it clicked off. Nobody said anything, which was a sign to Erika that nobody was paying attention to her, so to make sure everyone would know for certain that nobody, not anybody at all, including the president of the United States, should be allowed to sit in that middle seat tomorrow night, she said it again very loudly, and then when nobody said anything she decided her volume was too low and hit herself on the head. Then Frank grabbed her from behind and there was a mix-up, and after a long time she was lying on the cot in the health office. Mrs. Perry, the nurse, was next to her.

Jean was at the law center working on an appeals court brief when Mrs. Perry called. Erika had become a little hysterical during the dress rehearsal, she said, and her parents weren't available, and Mr. Janik, Erika's guidance counselor, had said she was Erika's attorney, so could she spare the time in her busy schedule to come?

"I'm on my way," Jean said.

The health office was full when she got there, but people

made room for her. "I'd like to talk to Mrs. Perry and my client in private if I may," she said, and everybody left the room. She looked at Mrs. Perry. "How is she?"

"Her pulse is one fifteen. That's high, but it was a lot faster when she came in here."

"Mrs. Perry, do you think you can give us a moment?" Jean asked.

The nurse left, and Jean and Erika were alone.

"Am I in trouble?" Erika said.

"You took something. What was it?"

"Accudane it's called. To help my memory. Only two. Three. That's less than the adult dose."

"Who says?"

Erika didn't answer.

Jean sat down on the edge of the bed. "Did you get it from a doctor?"

"It's from a drugstore, and there's a doctor's name on it," Erika said.

"But not your doctor, right? Maybe not anybody's. Are there more?"

Erika nodded her head. "In my locker. I'm sorry I got you out of work."

"You are my work," Jean said.

She stood up. "If the nurse says it's okay, I'm going to take you away. Might you have purchased it at one of our city's better thrift stores?"

Erika smiled and felt the buttons at her neck.

"Here's what's going to happen," Jean said. "You're going to give me the number of your locker and the combination, and I'm going to look in your backpack and return."

Erika started to sit up. "I can do it," she said.

Jean put her hand on Erika's shoulder and pushed her back down. "Stay where you are. Don't talk to anyone unless you have to. I'm going to send somebody for your street clothes. When you're dressed, I'm going to take you to my car and we're going to the emergency room at Saint Francis to have you checked out."

"Do I have to go?"

"Yes."

A half hour later, as they went by the open door of the auditorium, Jean saw a girl onstage with the book in her hands and guessed she was reading Erika's lines.

They got in Jean's car and started driving to the hospital. As they turned onto Young Street, Erika suddenly said, "I'm going to be sick."

"Right now?"

Erika nodded.

"Roll down the window."

Erika grabbed the crank and began to turn it. Ahead on the right was a furniture store. Jean drove around behind, where there was a Dumpster and some bushes. She jumped out to help Erika, but it was too late. The girl leaned as far out the window as she could. Jean opened the back door and dug around for a box of Kleenex, which she finally found on the floor. Erika had pulled her head back in and was leaning against the headrest, sweat on her forehead. "I'm sorry," she panted. "I messed up the side of your car."

"That's what car washes are for," Jean said. "How do you feel?"

"Okay."

"Really?"

"Really."

Jean got back in and drove around to the front of the store so she could look at Erika in the light from the furniture store window.

"You've got your color back."

"I ate too much lunch."

"And other things," Jean said.

A few minutes later she turned into the emergency room parking area at Saint Francis and shut off the engine.

"Please," Erika said. "I don't need to go in there. They'll see I'm fine and they'll put me at the end of the line and we'll be there all night waiting. Couldn't we go back to Dad's, please?"

"We're going to go in, Erika," Jean said. "Emergency rooms don't usually have patients show up with their attorneys. I'll do everything I can to make that count. It's the best I can do."

"You don't have to tell my parents, do you?"

"No," Jean said, "I don't. What your school does is up to them."

At ten, they were sitting in Jean's car across from Erika's dad's apartment.

"Tomorrow when you wake up, I want you to call me on the cell phone," Jean said. "You'll tell me how you feel. No 'I'm fine I'm fine I'm fine.' The plain truth."

"I am fine."

Suddenly the New York edge was back in Jean's voice. "I don't want to hear that now. Call me before you do anything else. You can go to the bathroom first. Could somebody else play your part? There was a girl onstage holding a script when we left school."

"I don't think so," Erika said.

"Good. I'm going to stay right here until you get into your apartment. Come to the front window so I can see you, and then I'll go. And don't study your part. You know it. Go to bed."

29

The next morning, Jean had her ear tuned for Erika's call. It came while she was standing with Christa at the bus stop.

"I know I'm not supposed to say I'm fine," Erika said, "but I'm fine."

"Shall I call the school? Mr. Stork? Anybody?"

"I don't think so."

"Good. You know I won't see the play until Saturday night. So break a leg."

When Erika got to school she went first to Mr. Janik in the guidance office.

He smiled at her. "It must be very nice to have your own lawyer at your age," he said. "She came to see me. We're friends. She just walked into the health office and took over, didn't she? What can I do for the star of the show?"

"I need a hall pass to see Mrs. Fine about my costumes," Erika said.

"That seems like a good reason," he said, and wrote her one.

She went into the girls' dressing room, turned on the light, and looked to make sure her first-act costume was back. Then she sat down at the long makeup table and looked at her face in the mirror. She wanted to see if she looked older, which she thought she should, but she looked about the same as always.

She considered spending the whole day in the dressing room but decided she had to go to classes as if nothing had happened. The Stork was waiting outside her homeroom door. He looked at Erika wide-eyed.

"How are you?" he asked.

"Fine. I'm sorry about what happened."

He led her to the band room. All around was the usual collection of folding chairs and music stands. Sunlight was coming through the windows, making the room too bright. She didn't know if she should sit down, so she kept standing.

"I'm not here to give you a hard time," he said.

"I'm sorry about yesterday, what I did."

"What's done is done," the Stork said. "You look okay."

"Really, I am."

"You're not a Hughie. You remember the kid who ruined *Arsenic and Old Lace* for all the other actors?"

She nodded her head.

"You know all your lines and what to do. You've got it all down. Some of the kids may be worried, but I'm not."

She knew he was lying.

"So what do you think?" he said. "You're ready, right?"

"Yes."

He waved her back to her room.

Frank came over to her at lunch period and asked Erika if she was okay.

"Thanks," she said.

"What for?"

"Stopping me hitting myself on the head."

"It was a mosquito you were fighting. Don't worry, I killed it."

"Thanks."

"No problem. Things like that are supposed to happen at dress rehearsal so everything can go right opening night. End of story." He waved and walked back to the guys he had been eating lunch with.

When she got back to Dad's after school she dialed home and rang twice, and when Mom called back, she asked for Karen.

"Hello?"

"Karen, I need to get you to do me a favor."

"Sure," Karen said. "Bernie's forgiven me by the way, as if you care, so you'll be able to watch TV all the time when you move in. You got to start being nicer to him. So, what do you want?"

"Was he mad at you?" Erika asked.

"I didn't have the right attitude, but now I do. He's coming to the show. He loves plays. We're leaving here an hour ahead. We'll be there forty-five minutes ahead so we can get seats front row center. Your dad's still working Thursday nights, right, so he's not going to be there? Bernie might be coming. He's just a small fish trying to get ahead like the rest of us, you know. So, what do you want me to do?"

"Mom told me she was going to bring the camera, and I know she'll try to take pictures while the play's going on. They'll make this announcement at the beginning not to do it with a flash, but she's probably going to do it anyway. I want you to take the batteries out of her camera so she can't."

Karen didn't say anything.

"Karen? Are you still there?" Erika asked.

"You know what, Erika, you've been trying to run the world according to your plan ever since you were three. Don't say it's not true. I was there. Quit it, okay? Just stop doing it. I'm not going to get Mom to leave her camera home, and I'm not going to take the batteries out, okay? Take care of yourself and let others take care of themselves. What else?"

"Nothing."

"Okay, goodbye. Oh, good luck tonight."

Erika skipped dinner. At five minutes to eight she was waiting offstage with the rest. All the lights went down except the orange ones in the side lamps, the audience got very still, and the curtain opened on the living room of the Winslow house in London with the family coming in from church. Sonia, as the maid, began to take their coats. Erika stepped through the door and gave her first line. The play was on its way. Five minutes into the first act she stood alone looking out the garden door. Her mother said something about the rain and she forgot her answer. Then she saw Frank standing offstage. He smiled at her, and she remembered it. She didn't forget a line or miss a cue or make a wrong move for the rest of the night.

When the show was over, she stayed in her last-scene costume and went to the front of the auditorium. She had never felt happier in her life. Standing next to the stairs by the piano were Mom and Karen and Bernie. She waved to her mom and went toward her. People smiled at her and told her how great she'd been. She knew they were just saying it because that was what you were supposed to say, but it felt good anyway. Frank bumped into her and introduced his parents. She could see from his mother's eyes that she was remembering the kiss and wondering how serious it was.

She got to her mom and hugged her.

"What an actress you are," her mom said.

Then Karen hugged her. She kept away from Bernie, and he didn't make a move toward her.

"I have to change and make sure everything's on the right hangers for tomorrow," she said, and went up the stairs to the stage.

Sonia was standing there in her maid's costume. "Everybody's telling everybody how good they were," she said. "With you it's true. You've just kept getting better. The Stork won't say it to you until Saturday, after it's all over, but I heard him say it to Mrs. Fine."

When Erika turned around, her mom was up on the stage. "I'll help you change, sweetheart."

"No, Mom, please. I'll be quick."

When she and Sonia came out, her mom was waiting. She grabbed Sonia and asked her if she had ever met Erika's father, and Sonia said no, she was sorry to say she hadn't.

"You want to see what he looks like and how he acts?" she asked. "Erika will tell you how I do a perfect Nicky Nevski."

She went to the doorway, put on a sad face, dropped her head, and held the pose. Then she smiled and looked at Erika. "That's him, right?"

"I don't think so," Erika said, but it was a lie. Her mom had him down perfectly.

"You know it's him but you won't say because you're a nice girl, but take a look at this." She went over to the ratty old wicker couch in the corner, turned around, dropped onto it, and looked up at the ceiling. "Nicky Nevski comes back home after a day at the body shop." She looked at Erika. "Right?"

Dear Diary,

I called Jean just now and told her the play went fine. I think she's going to worry until she sees it herself. She'll be sitting in the back row Saturday, she says.

The big thing is that I didn't let anybody down.

Mom and Karen came, with Bernie. The terrible thing is how happy Karen was. Bernie was mad at her, but now he's letting her watch his TV again. This is called slavery.

I'm going to go to bed now.

Love,

Erika

30

On Friday, Erika's dad came to the show in a suit and tie, which made him the best-dressed man there. After the performance he told Erika he had sold two tickets to his boss, who said he was going to come and bring his wife. He hadn't seen them, but that didn't mean they hadn't come. It was a big crowd, bigger than Thursday. Erika got Frank and Sonia and introduced them to him. Her dad invited them out for ice cream, but in the end it was just the two of them sitting in a booth eating hot fudge sundaes. He kept telling her how great she had been. It made her happy, but all she could say was that she was no actress and that he never would have known what she was saying without the microphones.

31

When Erika walked into the girls' dressing room on Saturday night, there was a vase of daisies on the makeup table with a card.

Dear Erika,

Kate is very lucky she's got you to play her, and I'm lucky because I get to see you both.

Love,

Jean

A guy from the florist's had delivered them backstage at five. Lucky for Erika, the Stork had been there to take them. At five minutes to eight, Erika went to the curtain and scanned the back of the auditorium, where Jean had said she was going to sit, but she wasn't there.

Jean sat in her car in the parking lot. She was in no hurry to go in. She'd walk in just in time and sit in the back corner, and if there were no seats she'd stand. It was cold, the first freezing night of the fall, and people were crossing the parking lot in a hurry to get in out of the wind. There were a lot of parents with their kids, the younger brothers and sisters of the actors. She thought for a minute that even if the play was dull she could have brought her kids, and she was sorry she hadn't.

Next time she would. She watched the red numbers on her dashboard clock. At five minutes to eight she put her hand on the door handle and kept it there. Her heart was beating fast. She was afraid for Erika. What if she went completely blank and all across the auditorium, even way in the back, everybody heard a prompter whispering the line? Well, there was no use sitting in a cold parking lot with her car door half open imagining terrible things happening to somebody she loved.

She didn't expect the play to begin on time, but it almost did. The announcement telling the audience where the fire exits were was finishing up when she stepped into the last row and sat down. For a minute after the announcement nothing happened, but the crowd stayed quiet. Mr. Stork came out of the door next to the stage and walked up the side aisle to his seat halfway back. Somebody applauded, probably a kid making a joke, but nobody joined in.

The play began. After the first five minutes, the loudspeakers on the right side of the stage started to whistle and then popped and went dead, so you could hear only what people on the left side were saying. When they moved to the right side, it sounded as if they were talking in a cave.

Erika seemed to be spending all of her time on the dead side, so it was almost impossible to catch what she was saying. Jean had seen the DVD of the movie version, so she knew the story, but still she leaned forward and strained to hear. The maid and Frank were the only ones who spoke loudly enough.

In the second act, they had both sides working again, but five minutes after the third act started the loudspeakers popped again, and all the microphones went dead. Mr. Stork walked quickly down the side aisle and went through the door next to the stage. A minute later the loudspeakers were on again, but then they went dead and stayed that way.

Then it was the last scene. The maid came in to tell about what had happened in the court, and the lawyer arrived and read the verdict of not guilty, and Erika went over to the fireplace and turned and looked out over the audience, and all of a sudden a deeper quiet fell on the auditorium, because everyone could see she was crying. For five seconds, ten seconds, fifteen seconds she said nothing, and tears ran down her face and fell onto the front of her dress. And then she stood straight and said the key lines, and even without the microphones they were clear all the way to the back of the auditorium.

Sir Robert—I'm afraid I have a confession and an apology to make to you . . .

I have entirely misjudged your attitude to this case, and if in doing so I have ever seemed to you either rude or ungrateful, I am sincerely and humbly sorry.

The kid playing Sir Robert was as surprised by her tears as everyone else in the auditorium. She took some small steps toward him and the front edge of the stage. She stopped and looked at the back row. What she had to say now was for her lawyer, her friend, her rescuer, her costume adviser, the woman she wanted most to be like.

I am not as strong as I pretend to be.

Then Sir Robert gave his next line, and Erika wiped away her tears and said the lines from the script, and the play went on, and then it was over.

The applause was thunderous, and when she took her bow, Erika was laughing and crying at the same time.

Dear Diary,

The show's over. Jean came and stayed around after, and when everybody was gone we went to the back and sat in the last row and she held my hand. She was worried about me missing the cast party in the gym, but I wanted to be with her.

So we're sitting there quiet and for a long time Mr. Dillon's going back and forth through the rows picking up programs and putting up the seats, and when he gets two rows in front of us he suddenly looks up and sees us and says we have to go right away, and Jean apologizes and starts to get up, but I say, This is my attorney, and we're having a conference, and he looks at Jean and she nods yes and he says I'm sorry and Jean says don't worry we'll meet you at the main doors at twelve, because she knows he's going to have to be there to let us out and reset the alarm system.

Smart lawyer.

So I'm sitting there thinking about what I said at the end of the play, and I hold her hand tight and say to her I meant it, I'm not all that strong, and if I go home I'll end up like Karen, and I ask her what she thinks I should do, and she asks me back what do I want to do, and I say I want to make everybody happy.

It's impossible, she says, which I know.

We get up and walk down to the stage, and we're both looking up at the Winslow living room, where I felt more at home than I have anywhere in my life, and I say to her that I promised Mom I'd come but I can't, but I don't want her to go into court and tell the judge that in front of Mom, and she says she doesn't need to, all she needs to do is tell him that I don't want to make a decision that will hurt anybody, which is true, and he'll know not to change anything.

So that's what she's going to do.

Then all of a sudden it's twelve and she drives me home to Dad's and gets out of the car and standing in the street she tells me that other kinds of cases get over and go away, but family cases just go to sleep until somebody gets mad and wakes them up again, and if that happens she'll still be my lawyer, and I tell her I love her and she saved my life.

I have to go to sleep. At ten tomorrow everybody has to get together at school and help clean up the stage.

Love,

Erika

P.S. Frank kissed me six times in three days. It was NEVER BORING, and I never pulled away before he did, and the Stork was wrong, nobody laughed.